MW00910289

# *Fiona*

&
*the Prince of Wheels*

# *Fiona*

### &
### *the Prince of Wheels*

## *Sandy Watson*

Orca Book Publishers

First Edition

**Canadian Cataloguing in Publication Data**
Watson, Sandy, 1945–
   Fiona and the prince of wheels

ISBN 0-920501-77-X
I. Title
PS8595.A858F5 1992   jC813'.54   C92-091185-4
PZ7.W37Fi 1992

Publication assistance provided by The Canada Council.

**Orca Book Publishers Ltd.**
P.O. Box 5626, Stn. B
Victoria, BC   Canada   V8R 6S4

Printed and bound in Canada

Illustrations by Terry Stafford

This book is dedicated with love to my brother, Jack, the clown prince and flying cowboy, whose wheels will never touch the ground again, but whose memory will soar forever on the wings of our hearts.

Jack Albert Blair, 1947 – 1991

# One

Fiona Malloy was soaring. She wafted through the morning mist towards the enchanted Land of the Unicorns with her sweater billowing out behind her like a sail. As the front wheel of the new bicycle splashed through a row of puddles along the side of road, she lifted her feet from the pedals, stuck her legs out wide and squealed.

"A genuine Race Rider Special, and it's all mine," she sang out loud. "Well, at least for the next fifteen minutes, it's mine." A gust of wind blew her ponytails into feathery strands of corn silk as Fiona pedalled faster. "Good old Taralin," she murmured. "What a buddy! I never thought she'd loan me her new bike on the first day she got it . . . ohhhhh!" The tires of the bicycle splashed through another puddle and Fiona shrieked with joy.

"Wish MY parents would reward ME for good school work," she said as she bumped over the railroad tracks, then coasted for a while, still talking to herself. "I could sure use a new bike like this to ride in the Easter Parade." A smiling Mr. Skipper waved from the top of a ladder as Fiona rode past his garage and read the sign: Spring Break Special for Student Drivers.

"Goood-eee! Eight whole days with no homework," she reminded herself. "Plenty of time to dream up my most spectacular idea ever. This time I'm going to win first prize in that parade, and for once I'll feel like one of the rich and famous."

She swerved to avoid a crow pecking at an apple core that had been tossed by the roadside, then puckered her lips in concentration. That reminds me, she thought, gotta phone Bradley to see if he picked up the black paper to make that Stealth Bomber for our science project.

Just ahead, on the sidewalk about one block west of the school, Fiona spied what looked like a fire hydrant with its fingers in its mouth. She pedalled closer until she recognized the chubby shape of her four-year-old neighbour. He hovered with one sneakered foot hanging over the curb, twisting his head from left to right, trying to decide if it was safe to step out into the crosswalk.

"Stanley Dregger, what are you doing way

out here all by yourself?" Fiona demanded.

The small boy straightened the seagull feather that poked up from behind his head and re-adjusted the strip of green material that he wore as an eye mask. "Mincha Turtles can go anywhere they want to go," he announced importantly, "specially if they gots their magic feathers on." He wiped his runny nose with the back of his hand and hunched his shoulders, cautiously watching the traffic whiz by. As a noisy cement truck rumbled past, he clapped his fingers over his ears to muffle the powerful sound.

Fiona couldn't help but giggle. She watched Stanley scrunch up his face and imitate the sound of the roaring engine. He reached down to give the elastic waistband of his baggy jeans a tug, then he jumped a little jump.

"Come here, Crazy Horse," Fiona said, waggling her fingers at the grinning boy. "You've got your buttons done up all wrong again." As her fingers brushed against a sticky blob of raspberry jam on the empty button hole under his dimpled chin, Fiona cringed. She quickly rebuttoned the rest of the row. "What are you doing playing on the main street in your pajama tops?"

"My mom was s'posed ta bring me ta the museem fer Jimmy's birfday pardy, but she gots the flu and she sleeped in, so ... I'm bringin' myself."

"Uh uh!" Fiona disagreed, shaking her head with vigour. "You are NOT crossing this busy street by yourself. Hop on. I'll give you a ride to the museum and we can phone your mom from there."

With one arm, she hoisted him up onto the rear fender. "OK, horsey, giddyup!" ordered the pint-sized Ninja warrior. He took hold of the pink leather seat and begged, "Be carepull ya don't sit on my fingers, Finny!"

Fiona walked the bike across the street when the light changed, then stood on the pedals and pumped hard to make her way through the enormous parking lot. On the far side, she could see the most unusual building in town — the only one with a giant antique car jutting out of its front wall.

They crossed the broad expanse of blacktop as Stanley peppered Fiona with questions. "Where'd ya find this bike? Well, why'd Taraling have ta get a pink one? Mincha turtles like green bikes more better, ya know."

Fiona huffed and puffed as they rode along beside the row of street lamps that ringed the lot. Her legs were beginning to ache. It was hard enough to pedal that long block from the corner to the Transportation

Museum, but what made it worse was trying to keep the bike from wobbling every time Stanley yelled "Faster!" and flapped his legs like a rodeo rider spurring a bucking bronco. Each lamp post they passed became an enemy as he whipped out his imaginary sword, waved it in the air and yelled "Take that, Shredder!"

They coasted down the middle of a row of parked vehicles until a tour bus beeped behind them. Fiona swerved to the right, pedalling faster to get out of the way. It was difficult to stay on course with Stanley flailing about on the back fender, but Fiona aimed for the main entrance and kept pumping the pedals.

Suddenly, the pavement dipped slightly and the wheels of the bike skittered over a string of pebbles. Stanley felt the bicycle shudder and yelled "Whooaa!" but they were going too fast to stop.

Just then, the museum door swung open and a boy in a wheelchair rolled out on a direct collision course. Fiona squeezed the hand brakes and rammed her foot down on the right pedal, but the tires skidded sideways in a puddle. Smash! Her front wheel slammed into the open door, knocking Fiona, Stanley and the careening bicycle to the ground.

When the door rebounded, it bumped the elbow of the boy in the wheelchair and sent the box he had been carrying hurtling into the air, scattering its contents all over the pavement. Stanley landed on his backside in a low juniper bush beside the wall. The green eye mask drooped at a comical angle just under his runny nose and his left ear. For an instant, two little blonde eyebrows arched like teepees while he tried to decide whether he should laugh or cry.

When Fiona struggled to her feet, a silly, rolling laugh rang from Stanley's lips. "Lookit yer bum!" he cried and pointed. "It's all dirty, jist like you been sittin' in bear poop!"

Fiona's face felt hot. The cuffs of her green shirt were stained and the hem of her once-yellow cardigan now dripped with muddy water. She stepped out of the puddle, turned and hitched up the side seam of her denim overalls, twisting herself to look at her backside. She could feel the soggy wetness seeping through to her behind, but on the ground she noticed a much more serious problem.

The front fender of her best friend's beautiful Race Rider Special lay twisted in an ugly shape with half a dozen spokes snapped off the rim of the wheel. "No!" Fiona shrieked. "Not Taralin's brand new bike!"

# Two

Feelings of guilt welled up in Fiona's throat, strangling the sobs that threatened to escape.

Through the broken bicycle spokes, she caught sight of a collection of balsa wood pieces spread out all over the pavement. She raised her eyes and turned to see the dark-haired boy leaning forward in his wheelchair. "Are you OK?" he asked, rolling ahead a few inches to offer her an outstretched hand.

Fiona shook her head, fought back a sob and took a deep breath. "I'm the klutz who should be asking you," she replied. He smiled, bent sideways to take a closer look at the over-turned bike, and rested his hands on his thighs.

That's when Fiona noticed it. Below his pale blue rugby sweater, he wore a pair of perfectly pressed corduroy trousers that folded under where his knees should have been. The boy in the wheelchair had only stumps for legs. Another pang of guilt shot through Fiona's heart.

He gestured over his shoulder with his thumb and said, "You're never gonna believe this. The lady in the gift shop just finished telling me I was lucky to move here during spring break because I'd probably bump into a lot of kids my own age." He winked at Stanley who was shyly peeking out from behind Fiona's legs. "I don't think this is exactly what she had in mind, do you? Seems to me it was more like a crash than a bump, but then, I'm not an expert."

Fiona could feel Stanley tugging at her pant leg. He pointed towards the wheelchair and loudly pronounced, "That boy's got no feet. Where's the rest of his legs gone?"

Fiona flinched with embarrassment. She yanked his hand back, then squatted and shook her finger up and down in front of his nose. "Stanley Dregger, where are your manners?" she whispered urgently. "That is a terrible thing to say!" She glanced up at the boy in the chair and gave him a thin smile, but her eyes were full of pity.

The young man set the chair brake, and motioned for Stanley to come closer. "It's OK," he said gently. "Everybody wonders the same thing, but most people are too afraid to ask." He gazed directly into Stanley's eyes and patiently began to explain. "Let's see, where shall I start?" He smiled broadly and crooked his thumb at his chest. "Name? P.C. Gillingham, the Third. Pretty fancy, huh? Same as my great-grandfather in England where my mom lives."

Fiona listened politely while Stanley cocked his head to one side and squinted his eyes in a quizzical frown. "I know, I know, let's get to the good part, eh?" P.C. winked and then continued. "The doctors said that something went wrong before I was born and my body didn't turn out with all the right parts." He brushed his fingers along the fold of his trousers where the stumps of his thighs ended. "See? No knees, no shin bones, no feet. I can't tap dance, but I CAN play basketball, and go to school, and read and write just like all the other kids. And last year I raced my dad in the 10K Sun Run, and we crossed the finish line together. So what do you think of that?"

Stanley rubbed his hand over the tread of the wheelchair tire and beamed at his new-found friend. "Kin I ast you a question, Peachey?"

Fiona gnawed on the end of her knuckle, wishing she could make herself invisible. "Peachey!" she murmured in disbelief, then she silently issued a fervent prayer. Dear Lord, don't let this little monster say one more embarrassing word.

"You noodle brain!" P.C. laughed as he

ran his hands backwards over the wheels. He leaned his torso back until the front of the chair rose like a wild stallion rearing up. "It's Pee Cee, not Pea-chee!" P.C. corrected as he returned his chair to normal position. Then he ruffled the little boy's hair and flashed Fiona a knowing look. "First we sort out this mess, then I'll give him a ride, OK?"

P.C. handed the bottom of the box to the curious little boy and rolled forward to retrieve the top. Stanley bent over to pick up a long thin piece of wood and an instruction sheet. "What IS all this stuff?" he asked, as he gingerly laid the part in the box.

"Model airplane kit. The pieces are cut out of balsa wood to keep it light so it'll fly." P.C. gave him the top of the box with the picture on the cover. "It's going to look like this when I'm done, see? A Nieuport Special with machine gun turrets and all."

Stanley studied the photograph on the box and imagined himself as a pilot. He lifted the front of his yellow pajama top to wipe a streak of mud from the picture. "Wups," he said. "I kin jist clean this off fer ya, Peach." Then he puckered his lips and sprayed spit onto the stained lid, and rubbed at it with his dirty index finger. The tiny speck of mud smeared and spread into a much larger greyish-brown blob.

P.C. laughed again, then he realized that Fiona had been silent for a long time. She stood staring at the broken bicycle, like a sad-faced china doll with eyes of glass.

He wheeled closer and touched her arm. "I'm sorry," he murmured gently. "I really feel terrible about your bike."

"It's . . . it's not mine," she mumbled.

"Whaaaat?"

"It belongs to my best friend, Taralin. I only borrowed it. I was supposed to have it b-back there b-by now." Fiona chewed on her quivering lip.

"Relax. If she's your best friend she'll understand. After all, it WAS an accident."

Fiona wrung her hands, unclasped them and wrung them together again. Her eyes were still locked on the dilapidated bike wheel.

"Listen," P.C. said in a brighter tone. "Maybe we can solve this another way. My dad's due to pick me up any minute. We could load the bike into our van, take it home and get him to straighten out that front fender and the bent spokes. He's in training for his third bikathon, so he's got tons of bicycle repair stuff."

Fiona raised her eyes and a slow smile spread over her face. "You really think he could fix it?"

"Hey, when he hears how it was my fault for not watching where I was going in the first place, he'll INSIST on fixing it!" P.C. rubbed his chin and waited for her decision.

"Well . . . " Fiona said slowly. "If you think he could . . . "

Stanley handed back the complete model kit and climbed onto P.C.'s lap for his ride. He fidgeted from one side to the other until he felt comfortable, then he pulled his turtle mask back up and twisted it so the holes were centred over his eyes. The seagull feather sticking up at the back tickled P.C.'s nose, making him splutter, but Stanley silenced his protests and barked his firm orders. "Readyyyyy, go!"

Fiona held the heavy door as the turtle and his driver wheeled into the lobby of the Transportation Museum.

Once inside, Stanley spun around when he heard someone call out his name. A tall woman in a plaid dress was shepherding a group of children in party hats into the small viewing theatre on the other side of the gift shop. Stanley flapped his hand at a boy who held a sucker in his mouth, and slid off P.C.'s lap yelling, "Hey Jimmy! Save me a seat benext to you!"

Stanley raced through the gift shop, stumbled on the carpet and nearly knocked over a spinning rack of postcards. Then he turned and ploughed smack into the legs of the lady wiping Jimmy's sticky face with a handkerchief.

"Glad you could make it, Mr. Dregger!" said Mrs. Hilary. She clasped his small, soiled hand and shook it firmly as if he were a famous and important guest. "Thanks for bringing him over, Fiona," she called. "We'll see that he gets a ride home." At last she shooed the stragglers into the theatre just as the lights dimmed for the movie to begin.

Fiona glanced back out through the museum window and winced again at the sight of the damaged bicycle lying in the puddle of water. She breathed air in and out between her teeth, squared her shoulders and said, "Guess I'd better call Taralin and tell her the bad news." It was easy to get permission to use the gift shop phone, but as she lifted the receiver, her hand froze in mid-air. "Maybe I could just tell her I'll be a little bit late bringing her bike back . . . "

P.C. sensed Fiona's discomfort. He wheeled away to give her some privacy, making a beeline for the middle counter, where he looked up to inspect the intricate Wonkeydonk model that hung overhead.

Back at the cash desk, the gift shop volunteer

counted out a roll of pennies. Behind the desk, Fiona cleared her throat, but she could not summon the courage to make that awkward call. Instead, she dialed Stanley's house and told Mrs. Dregger he had arrived safely at the party and that Jimmy's mother would bring him home.

Just after she hung up, a car horn beeped three times outside. "That's my dad's signal," P.C. declared, as he wheeled his chair towards the window. "Let me ask him if he's got time right now to fix the bike." He rolled out the door with Fiona close behind and veered left, where a burgundy van was parked with the motor running.

As Fiona approached the vehicle, a high-pitched beeping noise resounded from it. She stopped abruptly and stared, hypnotized by the action of a motorized lift that swung out from the rear of the van and lowered itself to ground level. The boy drove his wheelchair onto the lift and set the brake as a telephone buzzed from the front seat. "Dad's pager phone," P.C. explained, nodding his head in that direction. "He's a vet, so he's on call most of the time. Might as well load the bike while we're waiting."

Fiona nodded, but she waited another moment to watch the lift rise slowly and glide him safely into the rear of the vehicle. When she ran back to the overturned bike, the bent fender and jarring wheel spokes looked like ugly props from a horror movie. Fiona hesitated over the twisted wreckage. Then she took a deep breath, grabbed the pink handlebars and steered the crooked bike towards the van.

"If you can lift the front tire, I can probably pull it in here beside me," called the boy from his perch. "Dad says he can fix it, but he has to make one more call first."

Fiona propped one wheel up on the high bumper, then heaved. Together they managed to push and pull until they hauled the bicycle up and into the rear of the van.

A man's voice echoed from the driver's seat. "Sorry, son. Emergency call. They've got an injured horse at the racetrack. I'll swing back for you in about an hour, OK?"

"Sure, Dad," P.C. nodded. He pressed a lever to activate the beeping lift once again. When it reached ground level, he wheeled clear, then waited while it rose once more and folded back into the vehicle.

"All clear," P.C. shouted with both thumbs raised. As soon as the door whooshed shut, the van pulled away.

A flicker of hope brightened Fiona's thoughts. At least she was on her way to getting the bike fixed and back to Taralin. She shoved her hands deep into her overall pockets and was just beginning to breathe easier, when she heard a girl's voice call her name. "Fiona! Fin! Over here!" She turned and scanned the parking lot until her eyes registered on a familiar figure jogging towards them.

"It's Taralin," Fiona gasped, her cheeks taut with concern.

Taralin panted and puffed and scooped her silky black hair behind her ears as she slowed to a stop and broke into a cheerful smile. "You took so long, I thought I'd come find you." She nodded to the boy in the wheelchair and turned to pat Fiona on the back. "Lucky I saw your green shirt and your ponytails flapping in the breeze. How was the bike ride?" She swivelled her head from left to right. "By the way, where is it?"

Fiona squeezed her eyes shut and grimaced. She pictured her oldest and dearest friend as a walking time bomb, ready to explode. A horrible sinking feeling hit the pit of her stomach like an elephant dive-bombing a kettle drum.

Fiona stepped back and concentrated on the crack in the cement walkway. "Actually, this may seem kind of strange, but, I'm . . . a bit behind schedule because, uh, there's been a . . . little problem with your, um, with your bike."

Taralin's smile faded and her face turned

to stone. "What!?!" She locked onto Fiona's eyes and waited for the reply.

Fiona gulped, her mind racing at five hundred miles an hour. Start at the beginning, she thought, and go very slowly. "I was on my way home, going straight there like I promised, when I saw Stanley out on the curb by himself, and I couldn't very well leave him there, so I picked him up and brought him here, and then the door opened and I tried to stop, but the front wheel sort of bumped into it and some of the spokes sort of made a pinging noise, and then the front fender got this teeny, tiny dent, so . . . "

"A dent!" Taralin screeched. "You dented my new bike!" She planted her fists firmly on her hips while angry tears welled up in her eyes. "Before I even had a chance to ride it out of my own yard, you wrecked my brand new bike! I can't believe it!" She growled. She scuffed at the ground then paced up and down in front of them, chewing her lip to fight back the tears.

Fiona cringed. She bit down hard on the end of her thumb, then reached out and put her hands on Taralin's shoulders to calm her. "It's OK Tara, 'cause we've got things under control," Fiona reassured her. "Everything's going to be fine, now that I've found someone to fix it . . . a new friend!" A

half-laugh escaped from Fiona's lips as she nodded her head towards P.C. and stretched out a forced, but tentative smile.

Taralin's eyes widened in disbelief. She shrugged Fiona's hands off her shoulders and shouted into her face. "You think this is funny!?! You scare the daylights out of me, wreck my bike, then you tell me everything's fine because you found a new friend!"

Taralin's eyes seemed to flicker, then burst into angry flames. "You did this on purpose, didn't you?" she yelled. "You were just jealous that I got a new bike to ride in the parade and you're still stuck with that rusty old hand-me-down!"

Fiona blinked, unable to understand how the conversation had become so twisted so quickly.

Taralin sputtered as the tears spilled down her cheeks. "I . . . s-saved every c-cent for a whole year to help pay for that bike. When I think of all those extra arithmetic problems I did to earn . . . you KNEW how much it meant to me!" She wiped her nose on the cuff of her sweater then looked up, seething with rage.

Suddenly, Taralin raised her fist within an inch of Fiona's chin and spat out her ultimatum, "Well, Fiona Malloy, you'd better have it fixed, just like new, and back here by tomorrow afternoon, or I'll . . . never speak to you again!"

# Three

Cold droplets of rain plopped onto Fiona's head and shoulders, sending an icy shiver deep into her bones. Misery seeped in through every pore of her body as she watched Taralin stalk away. Why had she insisted on borrowing the stupid bike in the first place? Now she was in danger of losing the best friend she ever had.

There was a moment of silence, then P.C. said in a melancholy voice, "Seems like I bring you nothing but bad luck." He gently nudged the back of her leg with the wheel of his chair and murmured, "C'mon, Fin. Let's go back inside out of the rain."

Fiona held the glass door open and they proceeded through. Inside the lobby, they were greeted by a large white dog with black spots who was straining at the end of his master's leash.

"Morning," said a curly haired lady, as she struggled to hold him back. The big dog wagged his tail and bounded forward at the sight of the children. Keeping a firm grip on his red collar, the lady allowed the rambunctious animal to pad over and snuffle Fiona's shoelaces. Two ponytails brushed the sparkling tiled floor as Fiona reached down and scratched the yawning dog behind the ears. A smile fluttered across her face and the muscles in her shoulders loosened.

P.C. wheeled closer, and the dog nuzzled his outstretched hand. "Do you mind if we wait for my dad in here?" he asked. "My friend just had an accident outside your door with a brand new bike and she's feeling pretty bad."

"Oh dear," replied the woman, placing a hand on Fiona's shoulder. "Not serious, I hope?"

Fiona nodded that it was, then tugged at the seam of her overalls and turned to show her soggy backside.

"Nothing that a little tender love and care won't mend," observed the woman. "I wonder if our vice-president can put a smile back on your face." She reached into the pocket of her jacket and pulled out a couple of business cards which she handed to the children.

Neatly printed on the little white cards were the words "Vice-President, Guest Relations" beside a dog's paw print and the name

"Blaze." Fiona grinned and held out her hand to shake the Dalmatian's raised paw. He cocked his head comically to one side leaning his snout against her leg and dribbling a long trail of spit across her pants.

"Tsk," the woman exclaimed apologetically. "You'll have to excuse Blaze. He's still just a puppy and he's all stuff and bother when he first meets a new friend." She bent over near the animal's head and cupped her hand to her ear. "Really? Well, I'm only the manager, but if you say so, Blaze." She stood up and winked at P.C., then repeated what she had "heard." "Because of your little accident in our parking lot, Blaze has authorized me to give you two passes to tour the museum."

She invited them to follow her to the entry way of the exhibit hall. A heavy velvet rope hung across the opening. On the other side of the rope, P.C. saw the relics of more than a hundred years of transportation history — stage coaches and Model T Fords, penny-farthing bicycles and sporty roadsters with running boards, a Detroit Electric horseless carriage and a khaki-coloured Harley Davidson from World War II. In front of the main entrance gleamed the garishly-painted yellow Rolls Royce that had once been owned by John Lennon of the Beatles.

"See that one over there?" P.C. asked as he pointed to the ornately carved carriage to their left. "It's an exact replica of Napoleon's coronation coach. How'd you like to be Empress Josephine riding along the streets of Paris in that?"

As Fiona leaned over the fuzzy rope for a better look, the manager handed her two sheets of paper. On the top of each page it said: "Guest Survey."

"If you'd like to jot down your suggestions on how we can make the place better, from a youngster's point of view, I'd be very grateful." She unhooked the velvet rope and waved them in.

Fiona tagged along behind P.C. like an awestruck student. She listened with fascination to the vast amount of knowledge he was eager to share about the history of transportation. They viewed hundreds of exhibits over the next hour and a half, all handsomely restored and dis- played with pride.

By the time they had completed their tour, the birthday party had left. A bus tour arrived with two dozen Japanese travellers who milled around in the lobby, waiting for their interpreter to negotiate their admission.

Fiona quickly filled out her survey sheet and deposited it in the suggestion box. P.C., however, chewed on the end of his pen and said it would take him more time to think about how to word his comments.

While Fiona waited, she paged through the guest book, marvelling at the faraway places that some visitors called home. She wandered back inside the exhibit hall to gaze again at the display of antique coaches. How she wished she were a princess in a glittering white gown riding through her kingdom with Prince Charming by her side.

Suddenly something strange caught her eye. A shadowy figure in a dark leather jacket and hat was climbing over a roped-off area in a dark corner behind the antique hearse. He lifted a tall, brown two-wheeler from where it had been propped against a side wall, leaned it against his skinny legs and pulled on a pair of black gloves.

P.C. wheeled alongside Fiona. "See that?" he said. "He's taking that old relic out back to the restoration shop where they'll probably do a little research on its history. They'll polish it up and paint it to look like it did in the good old days. I'd say, around 1910 or 11."

As the children watched, the dark figure steered the rickety two-wheeler away, but he did not take it back into the workshop area. He ducked his head low and guided the handlebars down the corridor between the theatre and the gift shop, directly towards an emergency exit.

In an effort to be helpful, Fiona called out, "Excuse me, but that's ... " All of a sudden, the shadowy figure sneaked a furtive glance backwards, smashed his fist against the bar on the far door to open it, mounted the bicycle and pedalled out of sight.

Fiona sucked in a long gulp of air. "Am I crazy, or did that guy just steal that bike right in front of our very eyes?"

# *Four*

"I'm going after him!" Fiona shouted as she broke into a run. "Tell the manager to call the police!"

P.C. saw her dash across the parking lot, pounding over the pavement, leaping over concrete curbs and dodging approaching cars. The bike thief pedalled furiously. He sped across the main road and up the street towards the library, with Fiona galloping behind him.

Inside, the manager telephoned the police, but after she explained to the dispatcher what had happened, she listened for a moment, said "I understand," and hung up. "There's a seven-car pileup on the freeway east of town," she said. "Every available cruiser's at the accident."

P.C. told her they'd report back if they could find out where the robber went. Quickly, he returned to the parking lot, and peered into the distance. Fiona's billowing yellow sweater was just going out of sight. P.C. aimed his wheelchair towards the row of trees where he last saw her and sped off in hot pursuit.

It wasn't easy maneuvering around the traffic barriers, parked buses and oncoming cars, but as P.C. rolled across the pavement, he gathered speed. When he rumbled over the crosswalk at the main road, he had to zigzag wildly to avoid a lady pushing a baby carriage. He zoomed back on track, barrelling down a side street, hoping his shortcut would help him catch up.

By the time he reached the library intersection, P.C. found Fiona out of breath, sweating and pounding her fist into her thigh.

"Lost him!" she panted. "He got . . . clean away."

P.C. pointed to a thin wet tire track coming out of the puddle to his right. "Ah hah!" he exclaimed. "Maybe not!" With his index finger raised, he traced the unusually narrow tread mark on its route down a paved lane. They hurried along behind it, heads down, but when the track veered left just past the phone booth on the corner, a cloud of steam puffed out from the vent behind the dry cleaners making it difficult to see.

"Where to now?" Fiona asked, searching for any sign of movement in any direction. "We're not too far from Dregger's bakery," she remarked, as she paced in front of a vacant lot partially hidden by a tangle of overgrown blackberry bushes. Through an opening in the greenery to her right, she saw a long gravel driveway lined with telephone poles. At the far end, a weatherbeaten garage sagged. The drooping roofline and faded paint gave the old building a sad, lonely look. And then she saw something move. On the big double doors, an old-fashioned Coca Cola sign swung at an odd angle, creaking back and forth.

A question jabbed Fiona in the ribs. Was the sign simply swaying in the wind, or had someone just brushed past it and knocked it into motion? Someone on a bicycle?

She tiptoed up the driveway a few feet and beckoned P.C. to follow. With her finger pressed to her lips, Fiona whispered, "Hear that?" He listened carefully, then arched his eyebrows as a male voice shouted, "Oh yeah! Says who?"

Fiona quickly pantomimed her plan. She walked her fingers in mid-air then held her hands to her eyes like binoculars to show him she wanted to move closer to investigate. P.C. poked his finger at her stomach, hooked his thumb over his shoulder and moved both hands forward, palms out.

"You want me to push you?" she whispered. P.C. murmured out of the side of his mouth, "It's pretty near impossible to steer this buggy on loose gravel. If you want me to come along, you're gonna have to give me a hand."

Fiona got behind him, hunched her shoulders and pushed until she found traction. Cautiously she maneuvered the chair up the side of the long gravel lane. As they approached the worn wooden building, the voices suddenly stopped.

Fiona slowed the chair to an almost silent crawl. When they reached the cement walkway on the west wall of the garage, a row of holly bushes plucked at their sleeves, warning them not to go farther. Another string of angry words erupted from behind the side door and a deep voice growled, "I'm outa here!"

Fiona struggled to drag the wheelchair back into the prickly hedge. Once she was crouched in the green hideaway, she rubbed the raw scratch marks on her hands and stared down at P.C.'s crossed fingers. Just then a black panel truck careened around the far corner, sped up the alley and spit gravel as it lurched to a stop beneath the Coke sign out front.

From their secret lookout in the bushes, Fiona and P.C. watched a balding, red-faced man in the driver's seat prop his smudged elbow on the steering wheel. He cleared his throat and spit out the window. As the man lifted his eyes to his left, he glimpsed the shiny spokes of a wheelchair sticking out of the hedgerow.

The stranger's eyes narrowed. In the silence that followed, Fiona could almost hear the sound of suspicion gnawing on the big man's brain. Suddenly the truck door creaked open and a booming voice roared, "What in the Sam Hill is goin' on?"

Fiona opened her mouth and began to hum "Row, Row, Row Your Boat," as loudly as she could. She bumped the chair out of the bushes, and stared straight into the eyes of the ornery stranger, singing as if she'd done nothing wrong.

P.C. grinned sheepishly and croaked, "Just looking for empty pop bottles, sir," while Fiona just kept pushing. She puckered her lips and warbled "life is but a dream." Gravel spewed from each wheel as they scurried to escape.

For one split second, P.C. glanced back. The towering hulk glared after them with murder in his eyes. He tucked his thumbs into his belt, making his arms bulge out of his undershirt like branches on an oak tree. Suddenly, he raised his fist. "Beat it, ya brats!" he exploded.

Down the gravel driveway they dashed, their hearts beating wildly as if they were mice being chased by a ravenous lion. They didn't stop until they reached Fiona's house on Shannon Avenue.

# *Five*

Fiona bent over double with her hands on her knees, trying to catch her breath. "That was . . . too close for . . . comfort!"

P.C. leaned back in his chair and heaved a big sigh.

"Whew!" Then he laughed and slapped his forehead with the palm of his hand. "Are we ever stupid! We charged all over town, almost got punched out by the Terminator's twin brother and after all that, we didn't find one clue to the guy who stole the museum's bike."

"Shoot!" said Fiona. She lifted the lid of her family's mailbox and peered into its empty shell. "No evidence, no nothing. Speaking of bikes, I guess we'd better get to work on fixing Taralin's."

P.C. pointed over his shoulder to a tiled roof poking up on the other side of the Malloy's fence. "That's our place," he remarked, " . . . the one with the red roof, 157 Gable

31

Lane. Meet me over there in about an hour and we'll check it out."

She waved goodbye and trudged up her driveway and into the house. The kitchen was empty, but Fiona could smell the warm scent of fresh sawdust in the air. The buzz of an electric saw reverberated from her father's basement workshop.

A stocky older boy in a grey sweat suit with a cast on his foot, limped into the kitchen with a plate in his hand and turned on the tap to rinse it off. He looked up to see his little sister slipping off her shoes at the back door.

"Do you think the day will ever come, in this millennium, when Mom will bake a plain, old fashioned, ordinary muffin?" Everett asked with sarcasm. He flicked one last walnut into the sink and watched it swirl down the drain. "You'd think we were suffering from scurvy or something. I know there's a culture somewhere on this planet that survives on a diet of crunchy granola, oat bran, seeds, nuts and berries, but it is NOT in North America!"

"Where's Mom?" asked Fiona as she backed through the kitchen with her hands hiding the stains on her rear end.

Everett eyed his sister suspiciously and followed her down the hall. She slipped into the bathroom and slammed the door in his face.

The sound of running water gushed so loudly, Everett had to shout his answer. "I think she said she'd be at her gardening club meeting until later." He knocked out a rhythm on the locked door and chirped in a syrupy-voice, "Dad's in the basement playing carpenter, so I guess you're gonna have to fess up and tell big brother what happened."

Fiona's voice echoed from the small bathroom. "Forget it, Ev. When I need to talk, I'll go to someone I can trust, thank you very much. Not someone who snitches every time I get into trouble."

Everett's mouth silently formed the letter "O" as he remembered that it was Fiona who had organized his rescue when he broke his ankle three weeks ago.

He waited until the water stopped, then leaned his forehead against the wooden door and thought before uttering his next words. "Maybe we could trade," he suggested, clearing his throat to cover the awkward silence. "You help me solve my problem and I help you with yours."

Fiona unlocked the door and stuck out her flushed face. "What are you, sick or something?" she asked incredulously. She tightened the belt of her robe and searched his eyes for signs of madness. "You want advice? From me? What happened? Did all your snooty grade six buddies suddenly move to Timbuktu?" From the basement, the sound of loud hammering began.

"Oh oh," said Everett, cocking his ear apprehensively. "Here we go again!" He brushed past Fiona, grabbed the first aid kit from the bathroom cupboard and took out a box of Band-Aids. "Be right back," he said, limping towards the basement stairs.

Fiona hung up her towel and rinsed out the tub, then headed for her bedroom. The steady, rather frantic, hammering continued downstairs. The thought of her father's determined attempts to build things out of wood made Fiona smile. She looked out the window at the lopsided birdhouse that he'd made for Mother's Day and giggled. "Only two bunged up fingernails on that project!"

She pulled on a pair of comfortable jeans, slipped a turtleneck sweater over her head and was just combing her hair when she heard Everett's knock on her door.

"So far, so good," he said as he clumped in. "Maybe he's learning." He propped himself on the corner of his sister's desk with his sore foot resting on the rung of the chair. "My problem first, OK?"

Fiona nodded, plumped up her pillows and sank back against them to listen.

"It's like that Star Trek episode," Everett began. "'The Trouble with Tribbles'? Remember those two rabbits I bought for my science fair project?"

"Uh huh."

"Well, they're multiplying like some grisly intergalactic plot." He got up and started to pace, folding and unfolding his arms in an agitated manner. "First I built new pens to isolate the babies, then I tried to separate the males from the females, but they just keep on having litter after litter!" Fiona's hand flew to her mouth as she tried in vain to smother a giggle.

Everett scowled. He plunked himself down on the end of the bed and fiddled with a tiny satin bow on Fiona's quilt. "Look," he pleaded, "you're the one who's always getting detentions at school for daydreaming and winding up in trouble for your wild ideas, sooooo ... " he locked his eyes on hers to deliver the clincher, "I was hoping you might be able to help me come up with some way to sell off all the extra ones."

"How many bunnies do you have to get rid of?" she inquired.

He pulled a sour face and muttered,

"Thirteen."

"Thirteen!"

"What are you, deaf? I told you, thirteen! They're rabbits. They breed fast, OK?" He walked to the window, pulled back the ruffled curtain and looked out at the hutch in the far corner of the back yard. "C'mon, Fin. Dad said if anybody can come up with a wild and crazy scheme, it's you."

"He's right about that," she said, tracing the veins on her left hand. "Give me a day or two to think up an answer. Right now I've got something more important on my mind."

Everett cast his eyes over her gloomy face and asked what it was, but the ringing of the telephone interrupted her answer.

From the basement, through the air vent on the floor, they heard their father yell, "Ow!" then he hollered, "Phone's ringing!"

Everett shouted back, "I'll get it!" He hurried from the room, his foot cast thumping all the way down the hall.

When he didn't return right away, Fiona wandered out to the kitchen where she saw him replace the receiver and head for the back door. He shrugged on his windbreaker and called out, "Gotta get over to the library right away. Mrs. Zeeback's got that computer book I reserved and if I don't pick it up today, she says it goes to the next person on the waiting list. See ya!"

"Wait a sec! What about MY problem . . . oh, forget it." Her voice trailed off as she watched him hobble past the window and out of sight. "Why do I let myself think he might ever become a fully-fledged member of the human race!" she grumbled, butting her head against a cupboard door.

"Keep that up and you're gonna need a brain transplant," said a deep voice, as the smell of fresh sawdust filled the air. Before she could react, Fiona felt two arms encircle her waist and a pair of lips blow a raspberry on the back of her neck.

"Daddy!" she squealed in a fit of giggles. She squirmed and reached back to tickle his ribs, but he jerked free from her clutches and cried, "Truce! I give up!"

Reverend Malloy raised her hand high in the air and announced, "The winner and still champion . . . " then his voice grew even louder, "Jemima Q. Puddleduck!" Fiona lunged at him again and had already lifted his shirt and wiggled her fingertips when he whimpered a plaintive "No! Please! I was only kidding!"

He sauntered over and opened the fridge, leaned on the door and rubbed his stomach.

"I am starving. Feel like lunch?"

Fiona's father foraged. He slid out the vegetable bin, shook his head at the wilted lettuce, two green peppers and a bag of parsnips. Next he peeked into the cheese compartment and pulled out a wedge of cheddar which he tossed over to Fiona. Finally, he carried a bag of grapes and a container of milk to the table, favouring his freshly-bandaged thumb.

Fiona brought them a plate of fresh pineapple muffins and sat down with her chin in her hands.

"Problem, Sweetheart?" her father asked, as he slid onto the bench seat and poured two glasses of milk.

Fiona looked up into his soft brown eyes and silently rehearsed her confession. "Two problems," she declared, holding her fingers in the shape of a V. "Big ones."

"I zee," he said gravely, in a thick German accent. Then he popped a grape into his mouth and cut a thin slice of cheese for each of them. "Kindly exblen zem vun at a time. Vich vun iz first?"

She took a deep breath and blurted everything out in a rush. "I borrowed Taralin's bike and busted it in an accident and if it's not fixed by tomorrow, she says . . . "

Fiona made a cutting motion as if she was slitting her throat.

"Ouch," replied Reverend Malloy. "That's a tough one."

Fiona scraped her top teeth over her bottom lip and dug a walnut out of her half-eaten muffin. "Daddy, I have never seen anyone get so mad! I thought, because we're best friends, that she'd understand, you know, forgive and forget?"

"What did she say when you told her you were sorry?"

Fiona took a sip of milk. She searched her mind, but her memory bank was empty. "Well, I didn't exactly SAY I was sorry," she recalled, "but Daddy, we've been friends since kindergarten! Tara knows me well enough to figure that out."

Fiona felt a flutter of guilt in her heart, but she wasn't quite certain what caused it to stir.

Reverend Malloy tipped his head to the side and looked at his frowning daughter. "Maybe Taralin thinks you're taking her friendship for granted. Put yourself in her shoes. How would YOU feel if SHE borrowed YOUR new bike, wrecked it and didn't even apologize?"

Fiona was stunned. "I . . . I never thought of it that way!"

He got up and playfully flipped the ribbon on one ponytail. "Sounds to me like you need to do a lot more thinking to come up with some way to win back Taralin's trust."

He carried the empty glasses to the sink and rinsed them under the tap. "Your mother has a poem somewhere embroidered on a pillow. It says: 'Friendship is like a garden.' You have to spend a lot of time caring for that garden or it'll turn into a tangle of ugly weeds and wither up and die."

One idea kept intruding in Fiona's mind as she pushed a remaining sunflower seed around on her plate. "If I tell Taralin I'm sorry, she thought, shouldn't she have to apologize to me for saying such nasty things?"

"You won't solve anything just sitting there stewing about it," he remarked. Suddenly, he looked up at the clock, put his hands on her shoulders and drew her to her feet. "Now, problem number two had better be quick, because I want to finish making those flower boxes before Mom gets home."

Fiona told her father about the bike theft at the museum and how she and P.C. tried to track down the suspect until the man in the black truck shooed them away.

Reverend Malloy ran his fingers through his thinning hair and took a deep breath.

"This is serious, Fin. You're lucky you weren't hurt."

He bent over the blue box at the back door and picked up Wednesday's issue of The Surrey Leader from the stack of newspapers that had been set aside for recycling. "I want to show you something that may change your mind about playing detective, Miss Muffet." He paged through until he found the article he was searching for and pointed to the bold headline: Bike Thieves Strike Again. "See this? Six weeks ago the police noticed a sudden upswing in what they call snatch-and-grab burglaries, you know, sneaking up to people's houses at night and stealing bikes right out of their yards? Apparently things have escalated." He spread the pages on the counter and propped up his elbows to read the next paragraph. "Monday night they broke into Appleby's Sporting Goods and cleaned the whole place right out! We're talking thousands of dollars here, not nickel and dime stuff."

"But Daddy we were only . . ." Fiona's father lifted her chin and gave her a stern look. "Listen, Sherlock Holmes, you're off the case, hear me? If you want to help, you can clip this CRIMESTOPPERS number out and stick it up by the phone. Then you can call if you see anything else suspicious, and win the reward and buy your father a new Ferrari!" He patted her hand and gave her a smile. "Now, no more snooping where you don't belong, understand?"

Fiona slowly nodded. He leaned down and planted a kiss on the end of her nose. "Sounds like you're going to be a little busy anyway, mending broken friendships," he smiled, "not to mention broken bicycles."

# *Six*

Fiona headed out the back door but stopped on the steps and scratched her head. On the neighbour's side of the driveway, she saw a tangle of blonde hair appear in the small, low-level door normally used as an exit by the Dregger's cat.

Stanley wriggled his shoulders through the opening and held up the palm of his hand as if testing for rain. Then he bellowed, "Nope. I don' need no sfedder, Mum."

Five minutes later, Fiona and Stanley had walked around to the crescent-shaped street behind Shannon Avenue to find the house with the red tile roof. At 157 Gable Lane, a wooden ramp slanted down to the sidewalk next to the front steps and a stack of empty moving boxes had been flattened and propped against the wall of the garage. In the driveway, Fiona recognized the burgundy van with the handicapped sticker on the windshield.

A tall man in jeans and a baggy, striped shirt stepped out of the garage. He smiled down at them, arched his eyebrows and tilted his head towards the disassembled frame of a once-perfect bicycle. Lying there on a sheet of newspaper on the cement floor was Taralin's front fender. Amazingly, the metal looked smooth again, but as Fiona inched closer she could see that the pink paint was chipped and scratched where the dent had been hammered out.

"You must be the owner of that slightly the-worse-for-wear bicycle lying helpless on my floor," Dr. Gillingham remarked.

"Yes . . . well . . . no." Fiona yanked Stanley's fingers away from the fender, and held his arms pinned to his side in front of her to keep him from touching anything else. "Not really. I mean, it was me who wrecked the bike, but it actually belongs to a good friend."

Fiona thought again about how Taralin must have felt and hung her head in misery. It was as if some mean-mouthed giant had crashed her birthday party, stomped on all the balloons, smashed all the presents and sat on the cake.

Dr. Gillingham picked up a pair of pliers and bent over the wheel rim where the spokes had snapped off. "Don't worry," he said kindly. "I'll have it shipshape in no time. Give me another . . . "

he checked his wristwatch, " . . . hour and a half and it'll be ready for the touch-up paint. Why don't you tell P.C. you're here? He's in the house finishing his chores. Back door's open."

Fiona and Stanley pulled on the screen door just in time to see the boy raise himself up off the seat of his chair, supported by his arms. He slithered to the floor and with his teeth, snatched up the drawstring of a huge garbage bag stuffed with packing paper. Then, using his hands as push levers, he scooted across the tiled floor on his stumps to the top of the stairs by the back door.

"Hi," P.C. muttered through his clenched teeth. "Wun yast djob to shinish and I'm done." He looked down at the landing, wiggled his eyebrows at them and said, "Shtand ashide. Coming shthrough!" Fiona yanked Stanley out of the way as P.C. bumped down the four steps with the bag in his lap until he came to rest at their feet.

Fiona's mouth flopped open like the lid of a step-on trash bin while Stanley exploded in a fit of giggles and hooted "Hoo . . . he slided on his bum like a baby, didja see?"

Fiona closed her eyes and shook her head in dismay. She shoved Stanley out the door and pushed him against the wall of the house where she whispered a stern warning. "Stanley, that was so rude! Didn't your parents ever teach you? Never, NEVER make fun of people who are handicapped?"

Stanley's eyes grew wider as Fiona fired off another outburst. "P.C.'s not like us. He HAS to get out of his chair and slide on his backside to do some of his chores, because he can't walk!"

"Who can't what?" a voice asked from behind them. Fiona spun around to see P.C. wheeling across the cement patio with a puzzled look on his face. Her hand flew to her mouth as she wondered how much P.C. had heard.

"Stanley can't wait . . . " she replied, trying to cover her embarrassment, " . . . to see the playhouse we're going to set up out of these old moving boxes!" she added, happy to have successfully changed the subject. "Who wants to be King of the Castle?" she sang out.

It took a few moments to haul the big cardboard cartons onto the back lawn and set them up like palace walls, but soon Stanley was engrossed in a game of "Let's Pretend." He scrambled through the tunnel section then entered the vacant palace. Stanley dashed from one wall to the next, pulling down the cardboard flaps to hide from "the bad giants in the forest." All of a sudden, he popped up again and aimed an imaginary bow at the cherry tree, like Robin Hood defending his turret from the Sheriff of Nottingham.

Fiona couldn't help but smile. Her eyes roamed over the tidy back yard until she recognized two green shuttered windows on the other side of the high wooden fence. "Hey!" she said, pointing past the tree's budding branches. "That's my bedroom window over there with the white curtains."

Suddenly an idea popped into Fiona's head. "Too bad we couldn't set up one of those phone lines with tin cans on the end of a long string stretched between both houses."

P.C. glanced from Fiona's window and back again to the window above his left shoulder where he could see his model of the solar system hanging from the ceiling of his room. "We can do better than that!" he declared. "Follow me!"

He wheeled onto the sidewalk and around to the front of the garage where he signalled his father to come closer for a private chat. They whispered, then Dr. Gillingham nodded and said, "Don't see why not, son. I have to drive over to the hardware store to pick up some paint anyway, so I'll see what I can find. Be back in a shake."

After his father left, P.C. wheeled under the raised garage door and over to the workbench. He reached down and lifted a wooden box from a lower shelf, brought it up onto his lap and began to rummage among its contents, obviously looking for something.

Fiona reached in and took out a metal spool and a circle of chain links from among the odd objects. "What are these?" she inquired.

He poked his finger through one of the holes in an old telephone dial and spun it in a circle. "Well," he replied, "these are some of the gears and pulleys and wheels and stuff that I collect. I like to take things apart to see how they work, then I put them back together in new and different ways." He pointed to an odd-looking contraption sitting on top of a rusty old filing cabinet and proudly stated, "That's one of my inventions."

Fiona stood on her tiptoes so she could see it better, but it just looked like a jumble of mechanical parts, hooked together with rods and wires and metal bolts.

"Hand me that plug, please," P.C. asked. "It's much more fun when you see how it works." The moment the plug fit into the wall socket, a whistle tooted and the strange machine sprang to life.

Gears turned to spin a fan blade that looked more like a propeller, which made a little yellow light blink on top of a kind of miniature ferris wheel that twirled up, over and around to the sound of chains chinking and clinking. Finally, a hanging basket carrying a ringing bell inched back and forth along a wire from one Meccano tower to another.

Fiona stood fascinated, her eyes aglow with excitement. "You made that yourself?" she asked. P.C. nodded with a satisfied grin. "You are a genius!" she exclaimed, squeezing her hands in delight.

He shook his head shyly. "Naw," he flustered. Then he held his palms up and looked down at his chair. "But I guess you could say I've become sort of a specialist in the world of wheels."

"Hey, Finny, lookit me!" called a gravelly voice from the other end of the garage. They turned to see Stanley, sitting in the trough of a fertilizer spreader with his legs dangling over the front rim and his hands on the side wheels. "Now I got a cart, jist the same as P.C.!"

They took one look at the copy cat and burst into laughter. "Stan," P.C. said "you are one in a million!"

After considerable rummaging, they located a pair of hooks and two matching pulleys, which P.C. held aloft like trophies. "Yes!" he shouted. "Now, Stan, old buddy, I need you to bring me that red hand drill from the peg board, and Fin, could you help me drag this extension

ladder out back so we can get started?"

Fiona stuck out her bottom lip, then asked, "Start what?"

"We're gonna hook up a communications link from my house to your house, so we can send messages, just like you said."

By 4:30 that afternoon, the entire Malloy family stood in the back yard, admiring the newly completed "telephone" line.

Stretched high in the air across the two yards was a blue plastic clothes-line wound around pulleys attached to the bedroom window sills with large hooks.

Fiona's mother took her hands out of her pants pockets and applauded. "Well done, you two! And anytime my dryer goes on the blink,

I can use your phone line to hang the sheets out to dry." Fiona scowled, but her mother gave her a quick kiss on the forehead and added, "Just kidding, Love. I think it's great!"

"Any man who can design an invention that will keep my daughter off the telephone deserves the Nobel Prize," said Reverend Malloy, smiling and shaking P.C.'s hand.

"I only dreamed up the idea, sir. Fiona did most of the work," he declared.

Everett was the first to hear the creak of the line as it jiggled and wiggled and began to move.

"Whoops!" he said, pointing up. "Incoming signal."

Reverend Malloy boosted Fiona onto his shoulders to unpeg the clothes pins and take off the piece of paper that had arrived.

"My first message!" she exclaimed before reading it aloud.

"Your chariot awaits. One repaired bicycle ready to be picked up — no charge. If you could, however, release my son from captivity long enough to help me cook dinner, I will be forever in your debt. Your friend, Dr. G."

"Yahoo! It's done!" she screamed, then dashed across the back yard, climbed over the fence, and rang the door bell to thank Dr. Gillingham for fixing the bike.

"You're more than welcome," he replied. "Where's P.C.?"

Fiona was crestfallen. "I . . . I was so excited I didn't even wait. I guess . . . I thought he was right behind me, but I forgot . . . he can't walk."

"Ah, but that's where you're wrong, Fiona. P.C. CAN walk." Dr. Gillingham stepped outside to join her and closed the screen door behind him. "He was fitted with a pair of artificial limbs just after Christmas, and he's been practising walking with the hospital therapist for almost three months. Trouble is, the manufacturer keeps making one adjustment after another, trying to get them to fit properly. Someday soon, I hope he can bring his first pair of legs home for good."

"That's wonderful!" Fiona cried, her eyes shining with joy.

Dr. Gillingham agreed. "It's hard for me to believe, but in just a few days," he said, "my son will finally be able to stand on his own two feet just like all the rest of you kids."

"He must be a little scared," Fiona said with concern.

"I wish," Dr. Gillingham answered sadly. "But that's another story. Now I think there's a friend of yours waiting to get her new bike back. Let me know how she likes it."

The doctor's bicycle surgery had been successful. The newly-repaired spokes radiated from the rim of the wheel in a perfect pattern like the centre of a kaleidoscope. The Race Rider Special showed no visible signs of an accident except for one fingerprint smudge on the fender where Fiona had checked to see if the paint was dry.

All the way to the Wong's house, she kept picturing Taralin's happy face the moment she saw her bicycle looking as good as new. Now things would be back the way they always were.

When she reached Taralin's, no one answered the door and the car was not parked where it always sat. Fiona propped the beautiful bicycle on its kickstand in front of the old haywagon that stood at the edge of the driveway.

"There," she said to herself, admiring the graceful lines of her dream bike. "Now the whole family will see it when they come home."

# *Seven*

When Fiona awoke on Palm Sunday morning, she stretched and breathed the fragrant air that wafted in from the open window. A playful breeze chased the sweet smell of springtime over the tops of the green grass and invited her curtains to dance. Somewhere, not far away, a red-winged blackbird sang a cheerful tune to greet the day.

At church, Fiona fanned herself with her paper palm frond and peeked over her shoulder to where the Wong family sat, two rows behind. Fiona smiled and waggled her hand in a tiny wave, but Taralin only frowned. Mrs. Wong put her finger to her lips and signalled for Fiona to turn around.

The hymn ended and the harmonious words of her father's sermon reached her ears: "But the glory of friendship is not the outstretched hand, nor the kindly smile, nor the joy of companionship. Friendship is the spiritual inspiration that comes when we discover that someone else believes in us and gives us their trust."

Fiona knew that that was the way it should and could be and she was determined to start off on the right foot again with her own best friend this very day. She would march right up to her oldest and dearest pal and apologize properly.

After the service ended, she mingled with the crowd on the stone steps of the church, looking for Taralin.

Fiona overheard Mr. and Mrs. Wong invite her parents to the greenhouse on Wednesday afternoon to choose new plantings for the church rose garden. Finally, she saw Taralin standing on the lawn near the WELCOME sign, pulling on her white gloves. Fiona sneaked up from behind, tugged on the hem of Tara's coat and gushed, "Bet you were surprised to find your bike last night, hmmmn?"

Taralin looked at her blankly and said, "What's this, another joke?"

"I'd like to apologize," Fiona said rather formally. Then she grabbed Tara's hand and pumped it and smiled. "So! Now that everything's OK again, want to dress up like twins for the Easter Parade? If we make really nice decorations, no one will know I'm riding my old rust bucket, and of course, you'll . . . "

"I'll be what?" asked Taralin. "Pushing a wheelbarrow full of busted bike parts?"

Fiona's brain clicked into gear. "You didn't see it! I brought your bike back last night, but you were all out for supper or something. It's fixed, Tara! And it looks just like new!"

Taralin heaved a huge sigh, threw her arms around Fiona's neck and squealed, "Come to my place and let's celebrate. I'll tell Papa."

Fiona felt warm and wonderful sitting in the back seat of the Wong's car with her arms linked to her best friend.

When they pulled into the Wong's driveway, Fiona's eyes scanned the area in front of the haywagon, looking for Taralin's bike. Her forehead wrinkled into a frown.

"I left it right there," she muttered as she tried to see under the wagon. "This doesn't make sense . . . " Her voice trailed off as she got out of the car. She walked in a complete circle around the haywagon, but the bicycle was nowhere in sight. Fiona felt a heavy cloud of worry hover over her head, shrouding the morning light.

Mrs. Wong checked the back yard while her husband searched the bushes near the porch. Taralin hung back by the car, staring at the spot where Fiona had pointed.

Finally, Mrs. Wong returned, took both girls by the hand and said gently, "I'm afraid we have to face facts. I think your bicycle may have been stolen."

Taralin yanked her hand away. "No!" she yelled, then she turned and marched six steps down the driveway before she spun and stood like a raging tiger. "Fiona!" she screamed. "How could you? First you took my brand new bike, before I even had a chance to ride it, and then you smashed it up! Now, you tell me you left it . . . unlocked . . . in the middle of the driveway . . . when the whole town is crawling with burglars! And I trusted you to take care of it!" She stuck her fists on her hips, jutted out her chin and sobbed, "Y-you don't deserve to be anybody's friend."

Fiona trudged home in a daze. Taralin's right, she thought. I'm no good as a friend. I was careless and irresponsible and I took her for granted. "No wonder she hates me!" she moaned aloud.

The mid-day spring sunshine made her head hot as she crossed McLellan Road, so she took the shortcut down the library's back lane. Just ahead, on the next block, a figure emerged from the bushes wearing a dark leather jacket and pushing a single bicycle wheel with a pink inner rim.

Fiona's pulse quickened. Could it be the robber from the museum again? And wasn't that the same coloured wheel from Tara's new bike? She broke into a run to catch up to him. As she charged across the road to follow him down the next lane, a horn blasted in her ear. Fiona turned just in time to see a car screech to a halt less than four feet away! The teenaged driver shook his fist and barked insults as Fiona caught her breath and mumbled an apology.

She dashed up the lane, afraid that she had lost track of the thief, but then she caught sight of a leather-jacketed arm reaching out to grasp the corner of a brick building.

Next she saw the heavy collar of his dark jacket. This time she was sure. It was him all right, probably looking for another place to rob. Just then, his head lifted and he turned to glance back.

Fiona stood in stunned disbelief. She recognized that distinctive fuzz of red hair even from a distance. Someone from her grade four class was stealing the bikes!

# *Eight*

Back at home, the bitter taste of sorrow and shock bubbled all the way up from Fiona's aching stomach and into her throat, making it impossible for her to swallow. In the span of a half hour, she had lost one friend who now hated her and another whose life had turned to crime.

When Bradley Newcombe and his big brother Shane had first come to Cloverdale School, they quickly earned a reputation as nasty bullies. Fiona thought back to the time they chucked rotten tomatoes at her and her friends on Halloween and the day she saw them crushing marbles with a rock. But she also pictured the afternoon, just a few weeks ago, when Bradley helped her rescue her injured brother when they were trapped in that half-finished house.

Fiona looked across the table at the empty chair facing her and remembered Bradley sitting there just last Thursday laughing and co-operating with her on their science project as if they would always be friends. Now everything had changed. She could never be friends with a thief.

Mrs. Malloy put the last plate in the dishwasher and looked at the clock above the stove. "Well, if you're not going to eat, you may as well leave the table. And stop chewing your nails!" She raised Fiona's hand and pretended to gnaw on her daughter's fingertips.

Fiona withdrew her hand and murmured, "You just don't understand, Mom." She pulled her ponytails around her neck like a scarf and heaved a huge sigh. "This whole thing was my fault. I've GOT to get that bike back to prove Taralin can still trust me . . . but . . . " Blankly, she stared at the vase of daffodils that graced the middle of the table. "I've been wondering . . . what if one of the suspects is someone . . . "

"Oh no, you don't, Missy," scolded Mrs. Malloy as she bent over her daughter's shoulder and held her, cheek to cheek. "I'm with your father on this one. Hunting through the back alleys of town for a stolen bike is too dangerous for a nine-year-old girl. You back off and let the police handle this, understand? And stop fretting! Tara's bike will turn up, you'll see."

Fiona escaped to the solitude of her own room and flung herself across her bed, burying her head in the pillows in frustration. She rolled over and gazed up at the poster pinned to the far wall. There, surrounded by a pastel coloured mist, a graceful white unicorn galloped free in a meadow where alpine flowers bloomed. How Fiona longed to slide down a rainbow and come to rest in a land where every day was perfect and all her dreams came true.

Through the open window she heard a robin's song and sat up to find him perched on her private blue line. Quickly, Fiona took out her notepad and wrote a message telling P.C. what had happened. Then she pinned it to the wire and sent it on its way.

Within ten minutes, the back door buzzer sounded and Fiona looked down to see P.C. sitting in his chair with a funny look on his face.

In a voice reminiscent of a crooked-nosed gangster, the boy in the wheelchair asked, "Did yez want me to catch de bad guys for ye? I t'ink I could find de bike for yez and pound de robbers inta mashed potadas!" He raised his fists and shadow boxed in the air, but Fiona could only manage a pretend smile.

"I'm serious," he said. "We can go hunt around town right now if you like."

"Can't," Fiona replied. "My dad says it's a job for the police, not for kids. But I do have a clue." She tapped her finger on her chin. "I better not say. Besides, you don't know him anyway."

P.C. followed as she sauntered down the driveway and reached up to the lowest branch of the chestnut tree to pull off a cluster of leaves. "Wish I could think of SOMETHING we could do to help solve . . . " Suddenly her eyes lit up and she announced, "I've got it! Let's make a "Wanted" sign with a drawing of Tara's bike! We can put it up on the Lost and Found notice board at the grocery store."

Ten minutes later, they were meandering around a corner near the main street of town. As they proceeded up the sidewalk past the Thrift Shop and the dentist's office, P.C. slowed his chair to a stop and pointed to a doorway. "Look," he said, "it's the new neighbourhood police station. What would your dad say if we just went in and asked how they were coming along with their investigation?"

"All riiiiight!" Fiona cried happily and walked inside.

The reception counter loomed over a row of comfortable chairs that lined the wall under a bulletin board crammed with information. As Fiona approached the main desk, P.C. turned past a low table where a coffee machine bubbled and took a closer look at the notices pinned on the board.

Among the posters of missing children, another sign caught his eye. CRIMESTOPPERS was offering a reward of $500 for information leading to the arrest of a ring of bicycle thieves. "$500!" he whispered aloud. Then he whistled long and low.

Officer DesLaurier introduced himself and Fiona soon learned that Taralin's bicycle was the twenty-ninth case reported that month. "Do you think you'll be able to find it?" she asked hopefully. The policeman propped his chin on his fist. "The chances of getting it back?" He stroked his mustache and thought for a second. "In one piece?" he asked, raising one eyebrow. "Less than thirty percent."

Fiona looked so dejected, the big man took a moment to explain. "These guys usually cannibalize the bikes and sell off the parts or . . . they paint them up and ship them to another region and sell them privately."

P.C., who had been quietly listening, wheeled over and pointed to the thick file under the policeman's elbow. "With so many cases here in the valley, there must be some similarities, though, right?"

"Some," answered the officer, warily. He

took off his eyeglasses, blew hot breath onto the lenses and began to wipe them clean with his handkerchief.

The boy continued, "Let's say there was this small group of community-minded citizens . . . " Fiona pulled a funny face, but P.C. shot her a dirty look and then added, " . . . let's say these responsible, older adults started doing a thorough search around town. Are there any clues we, uh, they, should be on the lookout for?"

The officer made the shape of a zero with his index finger and thumb. "All we have to go on so far is that there are two or three males involved and one of them was seen leaving the scene of the crime in a dark leather jacket."

Fiona's mouth dropped open. She sucked in a big gulp of air and let out a tiny squeak. Officer DesLaurier pushed a box of Kleenex across the counter and motioned for her to help herself. She grabbed a tissue and wiped her nose as if she were smothering a sneeze.

The policeman stretched, pushed his shoulders up and rubbed the back of his neck. "We're gonna need one heckuva lot more evidence than that to get a conviction," he declared gravely.

Fiona quickly thanked him, then she grabbed the back of P.C.'s chair and pushed him directly out the door. She continued at a steady pace, down the street towards the apartment building where Bradley Newcombe lived.

"Surveillance watch," she explained as she sped along. "No chasing. No following. Just waiting and watching. That way I'm not disobeying Mom and Dad."

"What are you talking about?" P.C. asked. He watched her hunker down behind a telephone repair truck across the street from a three-storey stucco building.

Fiona chewed on a fingernail, eyes glued to the far door. "I feel funny about saying this, but I think . . . that is it may be possible . . . that one of my school friends is involved in this bike gang."

"Nice friend!" P.C. joked, but Fiona thumped him in the arm. He rubbed his biceps and grimaced sheepishly. Fiona lowered her voice and told him what she knew.

As the story of Bradley's behaviour problems unfolded, P.C. shook his head in dismay. But when he heard how Brad had helped with Everett's broken ankle, he arched his eyebrows in surprise. Fiona wished she could focus the confusing picture puzzle that had formed in the back of her mind.

She sighed and considered one final point. "Of course, Bradley also holds the world record for number of paper airplanes made and captured during school hours. I have to admit, though, some of them are practically works of art. In fact, we picked paper planes as the topic for the science fair project we've been working on."

P.C. stared at Fiona as if she had worms coming out her ears. "You're partners on a project with a bully who steals bikes?"

"That's just it," Fiona said with a bewildered frown. "I thought he'd changed. But I guess I was wrong." She sank her teeth into her lip and asked, "What would YOU say if you saw him, wearing a brown leather jacket, sneaking up the alley like a guilty criminal and pushing a wheel that had the same pink rim as Taralin's bike?"

"If he really IS the school bully, I'd get my butt out of that alley. I sure wouldn't point any accusing fingers in his direction."

Fiona heard her own voice forming the words very carefully, "Wait a minute! If someone . . . " she closed her mouth, thought for a second, then opened it to speak again. "What if Brad was sort of hooked into stealing by someone else? Like his older brother!" Fiona's eyes lit up at the possibility of shifting the mantel of guilt off Bradley's shoulders. "What if he's not one of the

REALLY bad guys, but just sort of a helper, doing what his brother tells him? What do you think the police would do to him if he's only following orders?"

P.C. bent his head sideways. "Fiona, everyone knows right from wrong, even kids." He looked up at the flock of crows that cawed and flittered overhead. "I guess if they're our age, the judge sends them to reform school to get 'em back on the right side of the tracks."

Fiona envisioned Bradley in a striped prison uniform breaking rocks with a sledge hammer, while his brother Shane egged him on.

Suddenly the door of the building across the street swung wide and Bradley appeared, carrying a brown paper bag in his right hand. He stopped to zip up his jacket and take a stick of gum from the pocket of his torn jeans.

"There he is!" Fiona murmured out the corner of her mouth. "What do you figure he's got in the bag?"

P.C. released the brake on his chair and said, "I don't know, and I don't care, but I have a hunch I'm gonna find out."

With a purposeful stride Bradley headed up the street unaware of the two people on the other sidewalk following him from a short distance behind. He stopped at the intersection to wait for a light, and worked his jaw, chomping

his gum. When Fiona rushed up from behind and tapped him on the shoulder, he jumped.

"Hi Brad," she piped up, her eyes glued to the paper bag he clutched at his side. "Going somewhere special?"

"Fiona!" he stammered, pulling the bag behind his back. "I'm . . . uh . . . goin' to meet Shane at the museum. We're . . . we're workin' on a . . . sort of a surprise."

"I'll just bet you are," P.C. muttered as he wheeled alongside and poked his hand at the brown bag in Bradley's right hand. "Pretty heavy lunch," he prodded, noticing the pointy bulges protruding out from under the paper.

"This? Naw. It's nothin'," Bradley replied, shifting from one foot to the other. He blew a fringe of frizzy red hair from his forehead and wiped his nose with the back of his other hand.

Fiona tried a different approach. "This is P.C., my new friend. Just moved in across the back."

P.C. nudged her in the ribs and smiled. "You might say we're partners in crime, right, Fin?"

Bradley's nostrils flared as he observed the familiar tone between Fiona and the new boy. He focused on a gangly weed that sprouted up through a crack in the sidewalk. "You still want me to come over Thursday to work on the project?"

Fiona drove her hands deep into her pockets and rocked back and forth on her heels. "Um . . . actually, Brad, I was thinking that P.C. could probably help us with that."

Bradley gulped and swallowed his gum. Feeling uncomfortable with Bradley's cold stare, Fiona forged ahead on another wave length. "You should see the whirligig machine P.C. made out of old wheels and stuff! He's sort of an expert on things that move."

Bradley looked down at the wheelchair and the stumps that were P.C.'s only legs. "Yeah, I can see he's a real whiz at movin'," Brad snarled with a cruel, crooked grin. He stubbed his worn black boot against the tire of the chair and smirked, "As they say in the funny papers, kid, don't call us, we'll call you."

A molten river of anger boiled deep inside Fiona's throat. Suddenly it erupted all over Bradley. "How dare you!" she shouted, as P.C. backed away. She lashed out to thump Brad hard in the arm, but her flying fist struck the paper bag from his grasp and knocked it to the ground. As it hit the edge of the curb, the paper tore and the contents spilled out onto the side of the road.

Fiona gulped. On the pavement, beside the ripped paper, were two pedals and an old bicycle seat. "Oh, Bradley!" she moaned.

"Why'd you do it?"

Bradley's eyebrows knitted together in confusion. "Do what?"

She pointed to the bike parts and sighed heavily with disappointment. "You don't have to lie and steal just because your brother tells you to."

Bradley froze as if the words had stabbed him in the back. His face reddened to match his carrot-coloured hair. He locked his blazing eyes on hers. "Oh I get it," he fought back. "The moron with the bad reputation who flunked grade four is too dumb to hike out to the salvage yard and haul home a few cast-offs to make somethin' that might win first prize in the parade, right?"

He shot a cold glance at P.C., then watched as Fiona began fidgeting with her locket. "Once a loser, always a loser in your books, is that it, Fiona?" He swooped down, scooped up the saddle seat and pocketed the pedals. Then he kicked the torn bag high into the air.

Fiona clutched at his sleeve and stammered, "Bradley, wait . . . " Brad stood stolk-still, his back to them both.

Slowly he turned and his eyes bored straight into hers. "Forget it, Malloy. And you know what?" He brought his sullen face within an inch of her nose. "You might as well forget that science project, too. Wouldn't want the whole school to think you was workin' with a criminal, would we?" He glowered at her and sarcastically mumbled, "Thanks for the vote of confidence, friend!" Then Bradley stalked away.

Fiona watched his shoulders droop as the toe of his boot kicked the disintegrating paper bag again and again until he was out of sight.

# Nine

On their way back across town, Fiona and P.C. were each lost in their own private thoughts. When they cut through the mall parking lot, Fiona looked up at the supermarket entrance and muttered, "I almost forgot. We were going to put that notice up on the Lost and Found board. I'll just be a sec."

As she strolled ahead, pulling the paper from her pocket and unfolding it, Fiona caught sight of two grade sixers from Everett's class pedalling their bikes towards her.

"Hi Marybeth, Hi Lindy," she called out. The older girls looked her way but refused to acknowledge a lowly grade four pupil. They dismounted, parked their bikes in the rack and hooked a chain through both front wheels and locked it. "Bet we don't get more than seventy-five cents," said the girl in the polka-dot shirt. She swung a bag full of plastic soda bottles over her wrist and pushed through the door in front of her friend.

The second they were out of sight, Fiona detoured to the bicycle rack with a strange look on her face. "Lindy's bike looks like . . . Hey! It is! There's the Race Rider symbol."

While P.C. tried to dislodge a twig from the wheel of his chair, Fiona continued to inspect Lindy's bike, muttering under her breath. She circled around, then bent over the front wheel for a closer inspection of the spokes. "I wonder if . . . "

All of a sudden, Fiona felt a hand yank the fabric on the shoulder of her sweatshirt. She looked up to see Marybeth Wilson's angry face staring down at her. "Caught red-handed!"

Lindy pulled Fiona's arm behind her back and wrenched it until it hurt. "Little twirp was tryin' to break the lock and steal our bikes, weren't you, Malloy!"

"No!" cried Fiona. "You don't understand!"

"Hold it!" P.C. demanded as he rushed to Fiona's side. "I saw the whole thing and you've got it all wrong."

Fiona massaged her sore arm as soon as Lindy let go and spluttered, "I can't believe you would just pounce like that and accuse me of stealing! You didn't even give me a chance to explain."

P.C. wheeled closer to calm the storm.

"Honest! It was all a mistake. Fiona thought YOUR bike might be the one that was stolen from HER friend!"

Marybeth and Lindy put their heads together and whispered behind their hands, but P.C. kept talking. "Let's face it, you were all wrong. You can't just go around pointing the finger at anyone who LOOKS suspicious."

The two girls held another secret conference and reluctantly agreed that, since she was Everett's sister, they'd let things go. Fiona apologized, and so did the others and they parted company, still feeling grouchy and uncomfortable.

Fiona grumbled for the next two blocks. She banged on the side of a letter box as they passed the post office. She whined, "Come ON!" while she waited for the DON'T WALK light to change. Then she bounded on ahead. "Imagine thinking I would steal their stupid bikes!" she snapped. "What kind of a creep do they think I am?"

P.C. pumped his arms hard in order to keep his wheelchair ahead of her as they bumped up and over the curbs. When he spoke, his voice came out in short puffs. "Well . . . you have to admit . . . it looked . . . pretty fishy . . . with you fiddling . . . around . . . especially, next to their bike lock."

Fiona stopped dead in her tracks and

whirled around to face him. "Don't you remember anything Officer DesLaurier said? There's gotta be a whole lot more evidence than THAT before you can convict somebody of a cri . . . oh my gosh!" Her hands flew to her cheeks and her eyes bugged out.

"What is it? What's wrong?"

She breathed deeply and pressed her lips together, concentrating to unscramble the jumbled puzzles in her mind. "My dad told me to put myself in Tara's shoes so I'd know how she felt, and I just did the same thing with Marybeth and Lindy, and I can see! I see how they took what I was doing . . . the wrong way!"

"Well I'm glad that's settled," P.C. said, kneading the aching muscles in his arms. "I thought we were going to break the land speed record until you calmed down. Having no legs is bad enough, but don't wreck my arms too, OK?"

Fiona didn't even crack a smile. Her eyes held a far-off look again as she dusted off a memory and brought it out into the light.

From behind a nearby dumpster she heard the pathetic howling of miserable cat. "I just remembered," Fiona groaned, "this is not the first time I've made that same mistake." She cast a forlorn glance at the alley cat straggling behind her and whispered, "I wonder if Bradley will ever forgive me?"

# Ten

On Tuesday morning Fiona wandered into the kitchen to find a note on the fridge door.

*Your father's gone to the nursing home for his weekly "How do you do?" and I've taken Everett to get his cast removed. Your turn to finish the laundry, Babycakes.*

*Love and Hugs,*

*Momma Bear*

The noisy blaring of an ultralight airplane engine passed overhead, reminding Fiona to pick up the phone and call Bradley's number. She listened to Shane relaying her name, then heard Brad's muffled voice in the background, saying, "Tell her I'm not here."

Fiona stared listlessly at the phone. She hugged herself to keep out the cold sadness that was creeping closer to her heart. Quickly, she rang another number and when she heard Taralin answer with a cheery "Hello," she smiled.

"It's me." Fiona announced brightly, but the dial tone suddenly clicked on as her once-best friend hung up in her ear.

Even P.C. didn't respond when she sent him a message on their private line.

Fiona trudged down to the basement and unloaded the dryer, folding the clothes as her mother's note requested. Then, feeling lonely and dejected, she wandered back upstairs and out to the hutch at the far end of the yard. Today she would concentrate on coming up with an idea to help Everett sell his surplus rabbits.

Thirteen delicate, lop-eared creatures cuddled together as they curled up in a corner. Watching their soft fur rise and fall in their sleep, Fiona guessed they were dreaming of carrots. She spread her fingers through the holes in the wire mesh wall and murmured in a tender, low tone, "Did you miss me, babies? Hmmmm?"

One buff-coloured bunny awoke and somersaulted down off the sleeping heap. He hopped closer to the cooing voice, then nuzzled the tip of Fiona's baby finger with a whiskery, twitching nose. "Are you tickling me, you little dickens?" she giggled. "Finny's going to find you a nice, new home so you'll be snug as a bug in a rug."

She picked up the clipboard and pencil

that dangled from a nail in the wood and lifted the first page to see when they had last been fed and watered.

"Water! That's it!" Fiona cried and she scribbled a couple of sentences. Under that, she began sketching what looked like an oddly shaped boat.

A horn tooted twice, signalling the return of her mother's car, but Fiona continued to draw. Mrs. Malloy "yoohooed" and carried a bag of groceries into the house.

Everett ambled across the lawn, happy to have his foot free from its itchy plaster cast. "Hey, Fin, you'll never guess who I saw at the hospital," he called. "It was your buddy, P.C., and boy, does he look different!"

Fiona let go of the clipboard and held the pencil in mid-air. "What are you talking about?" she asked with a frown.

Everett smirked and waddled like a duck, then he smiled and answered, "Sorry! Promised not to tell." He lunged to avoid the swat of her hand, then continued walking backwards toward the house, so he could fend off her rising fury. "Says he's coming over at two o'clock, so you'd better be red-eeee!"

Fiona's face flushed pink and her ears felt hot and prickly. When Everett saw her reaction, he couldn't resist a final punchline.

"What's the matter, Fishface? Worried that Prince Charming might turn into a frog?"

The rest of the morning and early afternoon dragged by like the days before Christmas.

Finally, at one minute past two, the doorbell rang and Fiona stepped outside to find herself face to face with a different P.C. Gillingham, the Third. He stood proud and tall on his new legs and feet with his arms supported in two metal cane braces to help keep his balance. And he beamed from ear to ear.

"I've been waiting to say this for a very long time," he stated. Then he swept out his hand and nodded his head in a courteous bow. "Miss Malloy, would you care to join me for a walk?" A radiant smile lit up Fiona's face as she jumped for joy, punched the sky and yelped "Yes! Yes! Yesss!"

It was slow going at first, all the way up the avenue, but P.C. soon got the rhythm right and began to set a comfortable pace. "All those months of practise finally paid off," he said with confidence. "How about an ice cream to celebrate?"

"Sure," Fiona answered. "Shall we cut across the school grounds or is it easier for you on the sidewalk?"

P.C. stopped and set his mouth in a grim line. "That's it!" he groused, "Not one step

further until we get something straight! I know you felt sorry for me when I was in my wheelchair 'cause I heard you talking about it to Stanley." He extricated his left arm from his cane brace and rubbed his right elbow. "But now I can stand on my own two feet. So why can't you just treat me like anyone else?"

Fiona felt confused. "I thought I was doing you a favour!" she argued in her own defense.

He inserted his arm back into the support and made her give him her word. "Don't do me any favours, OK? I have the same problem with my dad. Just let me make it on my own."

They shook hands on it and proceeded across the school yard, though their pace had now slowed as P.C. tried to gain a firmer footing on the gravelly surface. From under the eavestrough at the back of the gym, a swallow fluttered out and swooped down over their heads.

Startled in mid-step, P.C. caught the end of his cane on a low iron rung supporting the monkey bars. Suddenly he toppled over, falling against the steel support post. Fiona bent sideways and grabbed him at the waist, but P.C.'s voice rang out like a shot in the clear spring air. "Stop! Let go of me! Fiona, if you're gonna be my friend, you HAVE to let me manage by myself, please!"

Fiona stepped back and dropped her chin to her chest. "Everyone needs help sometime," she muttered bluntly.

"Well, not me!" he shouted with a defiant look. As he struggled to right himself and hook his arms into the support braces of the canes, Fiona strode ahead feeling frazzled and at the end of her patience. Just then, she spied a figure in a dark leather jacket strolling away from her down the road towards the main business district. Every other thought was wiped from Fiona's mind.

"Bradley!" she hollered. "Wait up!" Suddenly the gangly youth broke into a jog and Fiona ran to catch up to him.

When she reached the alley behind the dry cleaners where he had hurried around the corner, Fiona thought she had lost him again. Then she remembered the gravel driveway with the old garage that had the Coke sign on the door. "It was around here somewhere," she said to herself. She caught a glimpse of P.C. ambling along the lane behind her.

Then, as a city works truck pulled away, the hidden alley was revealed again. They peered all the way down to the end and spied the old sagging building with the Coca Cola sign. "No black truck," P.C. observed. "Shall we just take one quick look inside before we go home?"

Fiona nodded and cautiously crept up the drive, hugging the telephone poles for cover from unseen enemies. P.C. struggled to stay in her footprints, wincing once when his cane almost slipped on the rough, washboard surface.

As they came alongside the weathered building, Fiona put her ear up to the side wall. No voices. Carefully and quietly, P.C. crossed in front of the double doors, but his head bumped against the bottom of the sign which creaked and shifted at an odd angle. "The coast seems clear," he whispered.

On the east side of the old building was a wood pile that stopped just under a small window screened behind a heavy steel wire. "Onward and upward," Fiona joked. She put her foot on the wood pile and pressed down to see if it would hold her.

P.C. leaned one cane against the base of the pile to steady it, while Fiona crawled to the top and kneeled forward.

"This screen is so thick, I can hardly see through," she called down.

In the bottom right hand corner, she poked her fingers through a small rip in the wire and rubbed until a viewing hole emerged. What she saw next nearly knocked her over backwards.

"Bikes!" she exclaimed "There must be

hundreds of them! On the floor, in the rafters . . . this is it! We found the hideout!"

P.C. kept his eyes on the end of the alley as Fiona, in a relaxed voice, made another discovery. "Hey! There's the bike from the Transportation Museum!"

P.C.'s voice suddenly sounded scratchy and strained. "Hurry up! Do you see Taralin's?" he asked. "Maybe we can go around the back and sneak inside."

First, they tried the big double doors at the front, but a shiny new padlock and chain had been hooked onto the door handle and bolted into the cement foundation.

Then, on the west wall of the garage, P.C. found a small side door. There was a lock on this one too, but it was so rusty that when he yanked on it, the hasp almost pulled out of the wood. Fiona scuffed around under the holly bush until she found a rock about the size and weight of a cannonball. After only two strikes, the hasp broke, and they slipped inside, pulling the door shut behind them.

A broad shaft of sunlight slanted down from the skylit roof spotlighting rows of hanging bicycles that made eerie shadows on their anxious faces. P.C. pointed up into the rafters where large crates marked Schwinn, BMX and COOPER Helmets were stacked.

From the crossbeams, tireless wheel rims hung from ropes and long bungee cords.

"They must have knocked over an entire sporting goods store," whispered P.C. "Look at all this stuff!" His eyes took in the workbench on top of which he counted about thirty cans of spray paint with many different coloured lids. Fiona tugged on his shirt tail and showed him a large piece of cardboard with the shapes of bike fenders outlined in paint.

"Psst . . . over here," Fiona hissed. "What's that by the wall?" She threaded her way between two long, narrow rows of motorcycles. Beneath her feet, she heard a crunching sound and glanced down to discover a trail of broken glass scattered across the dirty floor. "Careful," she warned, pointing behind her, "look's like somebody dropped a bottle of pop. Eeew . . . sticky!" She scuffed a pile of jagged shards out of the way and moved aside a toddler's tricycle that sat beneath the window. Behind it, propped against the wall, stood a pink Race Rider Special with a fingerprint on the fender. "Ta-daaa! Taralin's bike!"

Suddenly P.C. shushed her and the two stopped breathing to listen. "Thought I heard something," he whispered. Outside, the distant sound of footsteps on gravel gradually became louder. Fiona backed into a dark corner and crouched down behind the first row of motorcycles. She beckoned to P.C. to join her. As he brushed his back against the workbench, Fiona pressed her hands together and prayed, "Don't let anyone come in here. Don't let . . . "

P.C. clapped his hand over her mouth and froze. The heavy footsteps scuffed up the sidewalk. Then, suddenly, they stopped. Someone rattled the rusty, now-broken door lock. Fiona bit her tongue.

"Aaarr," a voice outside growled. "I knew it was gonna bust sooner or later. Gordie musta come and gone with another load already." The footsteps moved off in another direction and faded until a nearby door opened and slammed shut.

Fiona sneezed twice and rose from the musty, dusty floor to clamber past the motor bikes and over to the window. "He must have gone into that house over there," she whispered. "Let's just take Tara's bike and get out of here. I'll go prop the door open."

Fiona scuttled back to the side entrance and pushed her shoulder against the paint-flecked door. Behind her in the half light, she caught sight of P.C.'s shadow as he picked his way through the maze of parked motorcycles. He struggled on his wobbling limbs to keep his balance and to reach Fiona's side.

Suddenly her eyes widened as one of P.C.'s canes clanged against something metal. She heard him stumble, gasp in shock and tumble sideways. CRASH! The entire back row of motorcycles tipped over and thundered to the floor, pinning P.C. beneath them.

# Eleven

Fiona's nerves crackled and spit like burning bacon. She leaned down to pull one of the bikes off the heap of heavy metal that imprisoned him, but the pile creaked and shifted, and P.C. yammered, "Wait! You're gonna crush me!"

"I give up," she finally admitted. "We're going to have to think of some other way to get you out of this mess."

P.C. lay back, half sitting, his legs pinned with his right arm brace under a tangle of rubber and chrome. Looking up at the shadowy loft, he searched his brain for a solution. "Wait a minute," he said slowly. "How'd they get all those heavy crates up there into the rafters? There has to be a . . . Fin! Look up high, over there by the wall," he gestured with his free arm. "Can you see a rope or a long chain with a hook on the end?"

Fiona cautiously stepped over another

fallen bike and made her way in the direction he was pointing. "Wish I had a flashlight," she muttered. "It's too dark to see much of anything over here." She patted the dark shadows on the wall, until she felt her fingers close around a stout rope. "This what you're looking for?" she asked with a smile.

"That's great! Just release it from its mooring and bring it over to me. See how it's looped through the double pulleys up there on the beam? All we need to do is tie the rope through a couple of these big bikes and you can pull them right off me!"

It took three or four minutes to tie and knot the rope. Then P.C. tested it for strength before handing the newly rigged "hoist" back to Fiona. She reached up as high as she could and grasped the rope so tightly that the coarse fibres prickled the palms of her hand.

"Ready?" P.C. said. "OK, heave!"

Fiona hauled on the rope. Hand over hand she pulled it down, harder than she'd ever pulled anything before. Soon the sound of shifting and scraping metal filled the gloomy garage. The pretzel of motor bikes shook, and then they rose five or six inches. Fiona gritted her teeth and hung on for dear life. "Almost!" P.C. encouraged. "My other arm's free! Now my legs! Keep pulling!"

Fiona wrenched with all her might. She concentrated on the taut rope high above her head, listening as it creaked over and through the two pulleys.

Then she heard a strange, grinding sound and felt the lifting motion cease. "Something's wrong," she whimpered. "P.C., what's that noise?"

"Hold on!" he coached as he yanked his trousers down over his undershorts and unbuckled his new legs. Concentrating every ounce of power in his arms, he levered himself up onto his hands and wriggled backwards and out of the terrible trap.

"I'm free!" he crowed. "Now, slowly walk your hands back down the rope if you can." But Fiona lost her grip. The heavy load thundered down onto the rest of the pile again. This time the motorcycles on top were twisted at a different angle, about eight inches from the plaintive sound of P.C.'s voice.

From deep in the shadowy corner, he called out shakily, "D-do you think you could r-rescue my pants and throw them this way?" In a mousey squeak, he added, "Please."

P.C.'s trousers were bunched half-way down the discarded artificial legs that stuck out from under the rubble. Fiona lifted the limbs by the ankles, surprised at their weight and rigid, rubbery construction. But no matter how hard she tugged on the hem of his pants, she could not yank them over the heel of his sneakers because the false feet were fixed firmly at an exact right angle. Finally, she undid the laces and removed his shoes, and the trousers slid off easily.

"Whew," Fiona sighed as she stood up waving the pants like a flag. Then she grinned and whipped the grey cords behind her back to hide them. "Wait a minute, mister. Aren't you the same guy who said he didn't need any help?" she teased.

Once again, the voice croaked from the shadows, "You're right! I admit it. Now would you puleese throw me those pants before I freeze my butt off on this cement?"

She tossed him his trousers and politely turned the other way while he wriggled into them. "Pants on first, then the legs," she chuckled, "that sounds so weird!"

She bent down and grasped the artificial limbs, but one hard pull told her they were wedged tight just above the knee joint under the back wheels of three Kawasakis. Well, it's not like they're going to walk away by themselves, she thought to herself. "I think we need a little more muscle than you or I have to get your legs out," she stated.

P.C. suddenly sucked in a quick breath. He sat up straighter and held the palm of his hand in the single ray of light that sliced through the garage. "Ouch! Sharp!" he complained, surveying the floor with a worried look. "How am I gonna drag myself over all this broken glass?" He folded the flaps of his pant legs under his stumps and thought for a moment, then gazed directly up into Fiona's eyes. "I need another favour," he asked tentatively. "Think you can sneak out and phone my dad to bring my chair?"

Fiona fumbled in her pocket for her quarter, then looked down and replied with a wink, "No problem, Shorty."

P.C. snickered and sputtered, "You pesky little . . . ."

"I'm just treating you like you told me to," she said with a giggle, "just like anybody else."

And she hurried out the side door with both thumbs up.

# Twelve

Down the gravel alley Fiona flew, racing around the corner, behind the dry cleaning plant and down the next back lane where she slowed to a halt when she reached the phone booth. She racked her brain between gulping breaths, but could not remember the Gillingham's number. She was suddenly jolted by a knocking on the window behind her. She spun around to find Stanley with his face pressed against the glass and his lips splayed out like a jelly fish. Giving him a half smile, she began absent-mindedly paging through the G's in the phone book.

Phloop. Stanley slapped a sticky blob of dirty bread dough against the window. Then he peeled it off and plopped it from one filthy hand to the other. He squatted on his haunches and rolled the dough over a row of tiny pebbles beside his feet. Then he patted it into the shape of a cookie.

"Waisins," he explained solemnly as he

held up the gritty, greying mass for Fiona's inspection. "Wanna taste?"

"No! Now, get lost!" snapped Fiona, who was becoming more flustered by the minute. She put down the phone book and dug into her pocket for the quarter then dialed her home number.

Stanley stuck his dirty sneakered foot inside the booth and said in a singsong rhythm, "My dad says I can play out back while he works in his bakery, makin' s'more bread."

Fiona ignored his nattering and poked her fingers into the coin return as she counted the fifth telephone ring. "It's Wednesday!" she recalled aloud. "They were supposed to meet at Wong's greenhouse to pick up some rose bushes today." She reclaimed the quarter and deposited it again, carefully dialing the Wong's.

Taralin answered with a friendly "Hello." Fiona grimaced. Silently, she prayed, Don't let her hang up. "Tara, it's Fin," she said with exuberance. "Don't hang up! I'm in trouble." The words tumbled out in a log jam of excitement. "We found your bike in an alley behind the dry cleaner's in an old garage. There's a red Coke sign on the door. We need your help. P.C.'s stuck without his chair in the hideout, and I'm scared the robbers'll come back any time for their stuff."

At first all she heard on the other end of the line was silence. Then Taralin's voice cautiously formulated a question, "How can I trust that you're telling the truth?"

"Tara," Fiona insisted, "you have got to believe me! I'm sorry for the times that I let you down before, but I need you to get my dad on the phone or just tell him to bring us P.C.'s wheelchair right away."

Out of the blue, a horn blared behind her. Fiona jumped and turned to see a black panel truck chugging up the lane behind Dregger's Bakery. As it slowed at the corner beside the phone box, Fiona recognized the bald giant who sat hunched over the steering wheel chewing the end of a toothpick and belching.

As the engine revved into gear, the truck turned up the side street towards the back of the cleaners where the blackberry bushes framed the gravel alley. The alley!

Fiona shouted into the telephone, "It's the bike thieves! They're on their way back. Call the police!" She dropped the receiver and raced after the black truck, hoping to reach the garage and P.C. before it was too late.

# *Thirteen*

Fiona WAS too late. The ramshackle black truck was already parked up against the garage door under the Coca Cola sign when she dashed back into the gravel driveway. As the door of the truck creaked open and the bald giant climbed out, Fiona slipped behind a telephone pole and sucked in her breath. She clicked her tongue three times, hoping P.C. would hear her warning. She prayed that he would stay safely hidden.

The huge man leaned on the side panel of the truck and took a plug of chewing tobacco out of a small round tin. He looked up at the house behind the garage, scuffed his boot heel on the gravel, then leaned through the open truck window and honked. Two short blasts of the truck horn prickled the hairs on the back of Fiona's neck.

"C'mon, ya slobs!" the hulk yelled. "Let's move!" At that precise moment, a skinny young man in dark pants and a leather jacket and hat shot out from the back door of the building and thumped down the steps. Behind him, a short, burly rogue smoothed a bandage that stretched across his bulbous nose as he lumbered up to the truck.

Fiona watched the driver swagger towards the front door of the garage. She made a dash for the next telephone pole on her tiptoes and stood rigid, before peeking out for another look. The burly giant reached up and straightened the angle of the Coca Cola sign as his two seedy-looking companions came forward to greet him.

"Didja bring any smokes?" asked the short man with the sore nose.

"Just my chewin' tobacco, if you want some," the towering figure replied. He took the lid off the flat tin and offered it around.

Cautiously Fiona crept closer, slipping from one telephone pole to the next to avoid being seen.

"Whaddyou mean, who's got the key?" asked the balding hulk. He spat into the bushes and slugged the short guy in the shoulder.

The tall weedy thief squeezed the shorter thug's arm muscle and gave him an ugly smirk. "Whatsa matter, Herb, didn't yer Momma feed you no Wheaties when you were a kid?"

Herb wiped his bandaged nose, snarled and threw a punch that landed on the thin man's chest. The next minute the two of them were wrestling on the gravel like Tasmanian devils.

"I said, break it up!" boomed the big monster as he bent down to separate them.

In the midst of all the confusion, Fiona heard a smacking noise closing in from behind. She whirled around and found Stanley, meandering down the middle of the alley slapping an ever-expanding glob of bread dough from one hand to the other. He was totally unaware of the danger in front of him, and heading straight into the view of the three ornery burglars who were now grunting like wild animals. What would they do if they lashed out in anger at poor little Stanley?

Just as he passed about three feet in front of her, Fiona clicked three times with her tongue and put her finger to her lips. Stanley stopped, turned, looked her straight in the eye, and held up one hand. "How!" he growled like an Indian chief.

Fiona lunged, grabbed Stanley around the middle and lifted him right off his feet. They ducked for cover behind a huge Salvation Army recycling bin.

The bald giant finally yanked the squabbling

beasts apart. "Enough!" he shouted. "We ain't got all day."

He bent over, inserted a key in the lock and separated it from the heavy chain. Then he grasped the handle with both hands. With a tremendous groan, the giant pulled on the handle with all his strength. The big double doors shook. They rattled and began to rise, but so slowly it was as if some supernatural force were pushing to keep them weighted to the ground.

From the inside of the darkened garage came an ominous groaning, a heavy grinding of metal on metal. Then, a thunderous crescendo reverberated as every motorbike in the second row clattered and crashed to the floor like a line of toppling dominoes.

"What the heck?" yowled the beanpole in the leather jacket, staggering backwards in surprise. Herb protected his bandaged nose with his knuckly hands and stared in bug-eyed wonder. To his left, Gordo, the mountain man, gawked. He scratched his round bald head and scowled, "There's somp'en funny goin' on here."

The lanky one was shoved under the door and told to check it out, but before he could adjust his eyes to the dark interior, a big motorbike wheel swung from the rafters and clunked him hard on the side of the head.

Down he fell like an ironing board and he sprawled, unconscious, in a tangle of bicycles.

Stanley took his hands away from his ears to point out the reflection of a red and blue light flashing on the faded outer wall of the garage. As she turned to look, her shoulders drooped. A police car was driving right on by. It rolled past the end of the alley and didn't even stop. The two remaining fugitives sensed imminent danger and froze for a split second. Then they darted out of Fiona's view behind the truck.

All of a sudden, she saw Herb's white nose bandage bob up as he streaked across the front of the garage towards the holly bushes. Just as he neared the corner, a shadowy shape appeared under the half-raised door and hooked the escaping crook's leg with a long piece of broken handlebar. The robber stumbled, fell sideways and hurtled onto two garbage cans. He yelped in pain and struggled to his knees, but P.C. rolled out behind him, looped a rubber tire around the thug's ankle and yanked it high in the air. Herb roared like an enraged jungle beast. Blood seeped through the bandage on his nose and dribbled onto his split top lip.

Fiona heard the engine of the black truck roar into action. She could see the frantic mammoth struggling to shove the gear shift into 'Drive.' Fiona grabbed the big ball of sticky bread dough from Stanley's hand. She ran out in front of the stalled truck and, with all her might, chucked the wad directly at the cracked windshield. The gucky grey mass splattered smack in the middle of the driver's sight line as the sound of crunching gravel echoed behind Fiona.

She turned to see a police car screech to a standstill and block the truck's only exit. It was all over.

While the thieves were being handcuffed, Fiona and Stanley congratulated P.C., who was sitting against the wall of the garage, tucking the bottom half of his pant legs under the ends of his thighs. "Good work, partner!" Fiona said as she squatted down to pound him on the back.

"Not bad yourself," he replied grinning broadly. "How'd you like my little surprise?" He turned to show them how he'd set his trap. "Strung that long rope through a bunch of the motorcycle frames, then hauled myself up on those other two ropes hanging from the pulleys. I inched it along that track and rode over here to hook up the other end and booby trap the garage door lift."

Stanley jumped up and down and cheered. "And we crashed 'em and we tripped 'em and we bringed the poleese, jist like the cartoons, right?"

Fiona stepped back into the garage and looked up. A long red and white striped bungee cord with a hook on the end hung down from the rafters. "So that's how you rigged up that swinging wheel. It looked like you flung it from a sling shot. I think the guy's still out cold!"

After the police officers locked the men in the back of their cruiser, it was time to ask the children a few questions. Fiona sat Stanley in the gravel and showed him how to sift the pebbles through his fingers looking for gold nuggets. Then she and P.C. recited the details of the crime they witnessed at the museum.

When another horn tooted, everyone looked up to see Reverend Malloy park his car behind the police cruiser. He leapt out, ran over and lifted his daughter in the air, swinging her around like a toy bird on a string.

"Thank the good Lord, you're all right!" he said as she landed again. He kissed her hair, her cheeks and her nose, then he noticed P.C., who was sitting beside Stanley, making gravel roads for ants. "I called your dad," the Reverend told him, "and he's on his way."

Over her father's shoulder Fiona could see Taralin creeping forward and waving shyly.

She held her arms open wide and suddenly they were hugging as if nothing had ever changed.

"Did I do OK?" Taralin asked. "I gave the message to your dad just like you told me and he called 911. I'm glad you're safe, Fin. I was scared when you left me hanging on the phone!"

"I'm sorry for all the trouble I caused, but listen! Are you ready for a surprise?" She clapped both hands over Taralin's eyes and guided her into the garage. "Open Sesame!"

"My bike!" Taralin shouted. "You DID find my bike and it's OK!"

Dr. Gillingham drove up and unloaded a wheelchair from the van. "Thought you might like to see an old friend," he said to P.C., who backed up into the seat and patted the wheels as if it were a faithful old horse.

"You know Dad," he replied, "it's great to have my legs for special occasions, but nothing beats a great pair of wheels!"

Suddenly a flashbulb popped, and the girls blinked at a smiling man in tan pants and a vest full of pockets. He had two cameras slung around his neck and pulled a notepad and pen from his vest.

"Kit Donovan from *The Surrey Leader*," he explained. "Just heard the call while I was monitoring the police dispatcher and thought I'd get in on the action." He clicked the shutter two more times then turned his attention to the policemen. "Any idea when these stolen bikes will be returned to their owners, Officer?"

The corporal rubbed his chin for a moment before answering. "Well, let's see . . . first we have to tag each item to document the evidence; then we can proceed with specific charges on this miserable bunch of hooligans. Next, there's the advertising, guess we'll put one in your paper, so people who've lost their bikes can come identify them. Any not claimed will be put up for auction. Should take about a month, I'd say."

"A month!" Taralin gasped, then dropped her chin to her chest. "So much for getting it back in time for the parade."

P.C. nudged the back of Fiona's legs with his right wheel and said, "Who needs a BIKE for the parade, eh, Fin? Tell her about your secret entry."

Fiona snapped her fingers and opened her eyes wide with delight. "Taralin, old pal, how'd you like to join up with us and try for first prize this Saturday?"

Stanley draped his forearm over P.C.'s wheel and smiled up at him shyly. "Prob'ly ya want me ta help ya dec'rate, huh, Peach?"

P.C. ruffled the scruffy hair of his little admirer. "Stanley, you're starting to grow on me."

# *Fourteen*

When Fiona returned from church on Good Friday, she put her Sunday school papers in her bottom drawer, filled a plastic grocery bag with ribbons, strips of foil, scissors and sticky tape and took it outside. As she laid out her supplies on the picnic table beside the back door and waited for Taralin, she heard Stanley's scratchy voice coming from the Dregger's garage.

"Be carepull ya don't drip that paint on yer slippers, Dad, or you'll prob'ly get a lickin' from Gramma 'cause she gived 'em to ya fer yer birfday and they costed a lot of money, ya know."

"Son, if I've told you once, I've told you a million times, quit dropping things into the turpentine!"

"It's on'y a weeny little ant," Stanley grumbled. "I jist wanna see if he can swim."

Fiona peeked around the corner and saw Mr. Dregger slapping green paint onto the top of a huge, round piece of cardboard that he had shaped and tied around Stanley's tricycle to make it look like a flying saucer.

"Looks great!" declared Fiona as she stepped closer to observe the porthole windows Mr. Dregger had cut into the spaceship's side walls.

"It'll look a lot better if the B E A S T ever lets me get it D O N E," Stanley's father spelled out in code. Behind his back, his little boy squatted down beside the gallon pail and checked to see for sure that Fiona and his father weren't looking. Then, with deliberate care, Stanley dragged his stubby index finger across the green goo on the paint can lid and held it dripping in the air. He stuck his tongue between his lips in concentration, and drew a green happy face on the hubcap of his father's left front wheel.

Stanley began to hum. "It's a beautipull day in the neighborhood, a beautipull day for a neighborwood you be my . . ." With a confident air, he wiped the remaining paint from his finger onto his clean T-shirt, then stood back to admire his work. Stanley lifted his shoulders high and grinned with pride.

When Fiona caught sight of his amateur artwork, she gasped. Quickly, she grabbed the crazy painter by the hand and hurried him out of the garage. "C'mon, Horrible, let's leave your dad in peace. You come sit at the picnic table at my place and watch me make my decorations."

Mr. Dregger sighed, gazed up through the rafters and murmured, "Thank you, Lord."

For five minutes, Fiona pulled the rainbow-coloured ribbons against her scissors to make them curl, while Stanley pestered her with 101 questions about the parade. As soon as she unravelled two rolls of paper streamers, however, the tone of Stanley's non-stop chatter turned into an annoying whine.

"But I reeeeally neeeeed streamers, Finny, so it could look like smoke coming out the back of my spaceship."

Fiona heard the tinkle of the message bell that P.C. had attached to their line. She stood up and glared at Stanley. "Enough, already! I'll be right back. Don't you touch one single thing, you little green-eyed monster, do you hear? When I come back, I'll show you how to make your own streamers." But Stanley didn't wait for Fiona to return. He raced over to his house with an idea of his very own.

The note on the line read: "Can you come over? Dad says the hot dogs will be burned to a crisp any time now, and that's just the way you said you liked them, right? Bradley says he needs your opinion on his contraption before he and Shane take it home." The note was signed with a drawing of two wheels.

At 9:15 Saturday morning, the parking lot of the Transportation Museum was filled to overflowing with excited participants. Eight parade marshals tried to bring some kind of order to the crowds milling around between the gaily decorated bicycles.

Each entrant was given a number and told to line up while the judges finished comparing notes before retiring to their reviewing stand. The town Librarian, the Editor of the newspaper, the Police Chief and the Manager of the Transportation Museum took their seats at the judges' table and waited for the parade to begin.

Two police motorcycles flashed their lights and switched on their sirens as they headed out on the route. Leading off the parade was the youngest entrant who steered a miniature green spaceship with pride. From his perch above his flying saucer, Stanley — the alien — nodded and waved to the crowd lining the street. His corkscrew antennae were so long that every time he moved his head, they wobbled, sproinged up and down and almost

It was easy to see he had come from a faraway planet, because his skin was covered with green food-colouring and he wore a cloak that was made out of artificial green turf. As Stanley rode past the reviewing stand, the judges all smiled. No  one had ever seen streamers quite like that before. From the rear of his flying saucer, the grinning alien had attached four half-block long strands of white toilet paper which fluttered gaily in the wind as the green monster merrily pedalled by.

Behind him teetered a dozen or more youngsters on short bicycles with training wheels decorated with balloons and brightly-coloured tissue woven in and out between the spokes. The cadet bagpipe band came next, drumming out the beat, then the school-aged entries appeared, some with pieces of cardboard clipped onto their spokes so their bikes purred like running engines. The judges shuffled their score sheets and remarked on the excellent quality of this year's decorations.

Fiona felt nervous. She longed to win that first prize of a new Race Rider bike. She pawed at the pavement in the middle of the street, glancing at Taralin who was dressed as

her twin. They smiled at each other and waited
for their section of the procession to begin.

Suddenly, from behind, she heard the
firefighter's band strike up a tune. Fiona and
Taralin pranced like graceful unicorns, trotting
in front of the cheering crowd in snowy white
leotards and silver-grey tights. High above
each girl's forehead, glinted a shimmering
golden horn.

As Fiona turned to acknowledge the
judges with a polite wave, her long blonde
ponytails drifted sideways in the breeze. She

adjusted the blue rope that encircled her waist and Taralin's. They had agreed at the start of the route that pulling a silver chariot wasn't as easy as it looked, especially when that chariot was really P.C.'s wheelchair covered in aluminum foil. Inside the shining chariot rode the handsome, happy prince wearing a regal cape, a royal chain of office and carrying a sceptre topped by a crown.

"For cryin' out loud! Tell them to quit stopping!" hollered Bradley from his precarious perch atop his homemade unicycle just behind them. He back-pedalled and wobbled to maintain his balance, then he flapped two large white cardboard wings like one of the early aviation pioneers and flashed a grin at the judges.

Near the end of the procession, the Play School Rhythm Band played "Here Comes Peter Cottontail" as Everett sidled along behind, looking hot and embarrassed. He reached underneath his long white beard to scratch where the theatrical glue kept irritating his upper lip. "I don't remember this fool thing being so itchy in the Christmas pageant," he muttered to himself. A gust of wind whipped his sack cloth robes against his pant legs, but he held his head high and smiled graciously.

Everett turned, changed his grip and

walked backwards, so the judges wouldn't read his sign until the very last minute. He pulled the wagon around a small pothole and admired his and Fiona's handiwork. Inside the wagon, on a sea of fresh bulrushes, rose a chicken-wire cage, shaped like an ark and high above that curved a rainbow of multi-coloured ribbons and streamers. The parade watchers pointed and buzzed about the ark and the precious cargo it carried. Inside the cage, thirteen lop-eared bunnies twitched their tiny noses, wondering what all the chuckling was about. As Everett passed in front of the judges stand, he heard the crowd laugh and applaud him. He swept into a deep bow and revealed to the judges the sign that he hoped would solve his most pressing problem:

*Easter Bunnies*
*$4*
*Call Noah at Malloy's*

The last parade entry to return to the parking lot was an antique car put-putting up to the speaker's platform and puffing out white smoke. The museum manager helped the mayor down from the rumble seat of the 1923 Dodge, and a gentleman in a checkered jacket climbed up two steps to the microphone.

The man smoothed his flowered tie over

his ample stomach and spoke into the mike, "As Chairman of the Board of the Transportation Museum, I'm pleased to welcome you to our annual Easter Parade. Today we are celebrating the opening of a new exhibit, but before I go any further, is P.C. Gillingham in the audience?"

Everyone muttered with curiosity as two unicorns pulled Prince Charming's silver chariot to the front of the crowd.

Chairman Noble nodded to P.C. and smiled. "Let me read to you from a recent customer survey card. 'Dear Sirs, Your exhibits are truly excellent, but you forgot one very important vehicle that has been around since the 1600's. The wheelchair has even been used by presidents and kings. I think Rick Hansen's Man in Motion wheelchair tour around the world proved that disabled people have their place in transportation history too. "

P.C. rubbed his chin on his shoulder and tried to hide his embarrassment.

Chairman Noble held up his hand to silence the buzzing crowd and continued, "There's a P.S. . . . 'If you need volunteers, I'd be glad to come every Saturday afternoon and work as sort of a junior tour guide. You might be surprised at how much a young person like me would know about the world of wheels.'"

Fiona beamed at the handsome prince. The crowd clapped again as the Chairman stepped down off the platform and walked over to shake P.C.'s hand. "We'd like to thank you for your suggestion, son. And now I want to make a little presentation." The big man's voice carried without the microphone as he wound up his speech.

"Ladies and gentlemen, I am pleased to open our new exhibit of antique wheelchairs and to honour the individual who suggested the idea. P.C. Gillingham, I'd like to present you with this lifetime pass and to take you up on your offer to serve as our first official junior tour guide."

Dr. Gillingham made his way through the crowd to admire his son's new badge. "Atta boy, P.C.!" he exclaimed as he pumped his royal hand.

Mr. Donovan, from the newspaper, kneeled in front of the crowd to set up his cameras just as the winners were announced.

"First prize winner in the Annual Bicycle Decorating Contest is . . . "

While the judges handed over the name and number, Fiona and Taralin crossed their fingers and arms together and then, for extra good luck, they crossed their eyes.

"Number 71 — Bradley Newcombe!" The onlookers cheered.

The Museum manager leaned over the edge of the stage and held the microphone to Bradley's mouth and asked him to say a few words.

Brad wiped his nose on the back of his hand and ran his fingers through his unruly mop of hair. "This, as you can see, is a homemade unicycle and these . . . " he lifted one arm and watched the cardboard flap up and down, " . . . are my wings." The people laughed and applauded appreciatively. "This design is just like the olden days when men first dreamed about flight. It didn't work so well, as you can see if you watch the movie about it, here in our own museum." Chairman Noble nudged the manager and they both clapped and hurrahed enthusiastically.

Brad glanced at the gleaming black mountain bike that the Chairman now brought forward. "I'd just like to thank my brother, Shane, the guys in the aviation section of the museum, and my other friends, Fin and P.C., for helping me turn a bunch of old junk from the salvage yard into . . . " he took possession of his prize and lifted it into the air, "this brand new Race Rider bike!"

Fiona rushed forward to pat her partner

on the back, share his exciting victory and invite him and his mom and brother to join the Malloys for Easter Dinner. "You deserve first prize," Fiona admitted honestly. "And Tara and P.C. agree. Yours is the most original float in the Easter Parade in the past one hundred years!"

The front page headline of the next edition of *The Surrey Leader* made the whole town smile.

*Young Heroes Thwart Bike Thieves*
*and Share $500 Reward*

The accompanying photo showed P.C. at the Crimestoppers Appreciation Ceremony, Taralin and Fiona's arms linked over his shoulders. The grinning trio were singing an off-key, but heartfelt rendition of "That's What Friends Are For."

# *Acknowledgements*

Everywhere I go, I meet people who are so special, I capture them in my memories and often they emerge as characters in my stories. When my children were very small, we moved to Sherwood Park, Alberta. One day, across the street from our house, a boy appeared in a wheelchair, whistling happily and bouncing a basketball. That boy served as a wonderful role model for my children for years to come, helping them discover, for the first time, the joys of friendship. Despite the difference in age, he always made time for two pesky pre-schoolers whom he treated with kindness and patience, earning their love and admiration. They watched him take on the same responsibilities and chores as his brothers and sister so he would be treated as an equal with self-respect and pride. Jody Higgins, I thank you. Those memories of you inspired me to write this book.

At Silver Lake, Washington, another young man in a wheelchair provided inspiration, information and encouragement for this project. The quiet strength and determination of Luis Betts will spur him over the finish line many times in the next few years as he continues to break records in wheelchair racing and in the Olympic swimming pool.

To Susanna Sweeney-Martini, I owe perhaps the biggest debt of gratitude. When I visited her at Jefferson School in Spokane, Washington, this tiny angel opened her heart and allowed me a glimpse at the private feelings and secret wishes of a disabled child. Through her I began to understand the magic spirit and spunk that keeps the physically challenged focused on their dreams In the Land of the Unicorns, Susanna will always be my favourite princess.

I want to thank Merl Smock and the staff of the Shriners' Hospital for Crippled Children in Spokane who took the time to explain the nature of physical disabilities and provided me with infomation about Streeters Band Dysplasia.

Without the help of the reference librarians at the Nanaimo Regional Library, the Surrey Public Library and the Spokane Library systems, I would still be floundering for answers to so many questions like the origins of the wheelchair or how a double pulley works.

Special thanks to the staff and volunteers at the British Columbia Transportion Museum on #10 Highway in Cloverdale. You have created a special place where children and adults can imagine life in a bygone era and the wonderful world of wheels.